DARING PROPOSAL

THE DARE MÉNAGE SERIES
BOOK TWO

JEANNE ST. JAMES

Editor: Molly S. Daniels
Cover Art: April Martinez

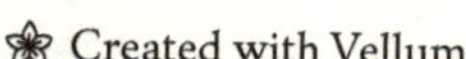

www.jeannestjames.com

Sign up for my newsletter for insider information, author news, and new releases:
www.jeannestjames.com/newslettersignup

❋ Created with Vellum

THE DARE MENAGE SERIES

The Dare Ménage Series:
(All can be read as standalones)

ACKNOWLEDGMENTS

Thank you to my friend, Dallas Cantland, drummer extraordinaire, and his punk rock band, Thorazine, for allowing me to use them and their lyrics in this book. You're a real character, Dallas, so you made it easy for me.

CHAPTER 1

"I'm so fucking sick of this shit."

"Tell me about it, Renny."

Ren Landis turned toward the voice behind him. He hadn't realized anyone was nearby.

His former Boston Bulldogs teammate and best friend gave him a wide smile and a quick slap on the ass.

"Why do we do this shit?" Ren asked Cole Dixon.

Cole gave a sloppy shrug. "Who the hell knows? Because we wanna give back?"

Ren snorted. "Give back," he repeated. He shook his head and sighed. "Right."

Poverty, cancer, AIDS, hunger, disaster relief… The causes were endless. But it was a way to give back. Cole was right.

He'd had a successful career. Made more money than he knew what to do with. He had respect from the public, his fellow NFL players, and, for the most part, the media. Imagine that. Him. Little ol' Lawrence "Long-Arm" Landis. Okay, sometimes the gossip rags, not so much.

The more he "gave back" the more he "got." His stardom hadn't ended when he retired at the ripe old age of thirty-two, which was young for a quarterback. No, charities helped keep him in the spotlight. He got endorsement deals, commercials, reality TV gigs, gifts, and women. Lots and lots of women.

So, he shouldn't be a whiny bitch complaining about spending an evening at a charity function. Though, he could be home watching *SportsCenter*. Or, hell, even *Dancing with the Stars*.

Ren felt a hand on his back.

"Whoa, where'd ya go?"

Ren shook his head again. "Nowhere." He did a fake-out punch to Cole's stomach. "Damn. I just want to get this over with tonight."

Out of all the charity functions he attended, he hated the "auctions" the most. The ones where he had to stand on the stage and strut his stuff. Where he was no more than a piece of meat. Where he went to the highest bidder, who usually ended up being some older woman who didn't know shit about football. Or some chick who only knew he was a famous "someone." Or a groupie who had enough money to "buy" him and expected more than dinner for her money.

"Not sure why Dan keeps signing us up for these things. I hate 'em too."

Ren didn't know why either. Dan was Ren's and Cole's sports agent. He'd told Dan he doesn't like the auctions. He would have to make it clear. Once again. Next time Dan booked him for one of these, he was getting a size thirteen foot up his ass. Good cause or not.

"Hey, Renny, have I told you your ass has been looking mighty fine lately, and that I miss standing behind it while you're bent over?"

Ren chuckled. He was used to good-natured ribbing from Cole. Ren was a former NFL quarterback for the Boston Bulldogs. A good one, at that. And Cole had been his running back—his right-hand man during his whole career with the team. Cole never hid the fact he loved sex and it didn't matter who it was with, man or woman. Or even both at the same time.

In fact, Ren was always envious of Cole's confidence in his manhood, his sexuality. Cole reminded him of another former teammate, Ty White.

Ty was in relationship with two lovers, a man *and* a woman. Running into him at a similar charity event about a year ago, he'd wanted to ask a million questions on how that all worked, but never got the chance. Nor did he want to pry too much into their private life.

But he was definitely curious. Who wouldn't be? Most relationships between just two people were hard enough. Ren was the king of failed relationships. But to add an extra person? He shook his head.

The sound of applause interrupted Ren's thoughts. He shifted to his other foot. He and Cole stood in a makeshift waiting area behind some curtains. The image of sharks waiting for chum popped in his mind as the MC's voice filled the area.

"Ladies and gentleman, we are happy you've all decided to come out tonight and support this great cause…"

Ren's stomach turned. Did he say he hated these things? He *hated* them!

He wiped his sweaty palms against his thighs.

"Brother, you can't be that nervous!"

"Shut up," Ren muttered, causing Cole to fall into a bout of laughter. And not normal laughter, but exaggerated laughter with pointing, guffawing, and even knee slapping. He was going to kick his ass. Right after he kicked Dan's.

"Renny, you're a freaking legend, man! You're used to the limelight!"

"Isn't the same."

"Are you serious?" The surprise apparent on Cole's face.

"I said shut up," Ren warned him. The guy wasn't making him feel any better.

"If you need to puke, do it elsewhere."

"I'm not going to puke. It's just some of these women are

relentless. Clawing at me, trying to unbutton my pants, sticking their tongue in my ear. One of them almost swallowed one of my earrings." Ren tugged at one of the large diamond studs in his ear.

"You love women!"

"Yeah, when they're bangin' hot! Some of these are scary! Beasts even!"

Cole slapped an arm around Ren's shoulders and squeezed. "Next you're going to say that you felt violated."

Ren wanted to wipe that shit-eating grin right off his face. But Cole was probably right. Ren was making way too much out of all this. He was only obligated to spend a couple hours with whoever was the highest bidder. If they picked a movie as the date, then it would even be better. Two hours in the dark without talking.

"Why are we the only fools waiting in this room? I need some air."

He pushed back the heavy black piece of cloth, which was supposed to be the "door," and stomped out before he could hear Cole's answer.

He strode down the loud, busy hallway, weaving through the male and female auctionees.

He received some pats on the back as people recognized him. He shrugged them all off and burst through the nearest exit, out into the warm evening, sucking in a deep breath.

A tinkle of laughter came from his right, and a small group of people approached him. It wasn't until they were under the building's security light that he could make out who they were.

"Renny! How about that? What are the chances of meeting you here?" Quinn Preston teased him as she approached him, flanked arm in arm by two men. One dark, one deeply tanned, both wearing very big smiles. Ren swept his gaze over Quinn from the top of her head down to her polished toes.

Sexy as shit. But out loud he said, "Lovely as ever, Quinn."

"As pregnant as ever, you mean."

Ren studied her very rounded belly and fought the urge to reach out and touch it. "Still beautiful. Congratulations, by the way." He leaned into Quinn, kissing her. He tried for the lips, but she turned her head at the last minute; his lips brushed her cheek instead. He laughed as he pulled back. Ty would consider the attempt funny. Logan not so much. And that's exactly why he did it. There was a twinkle in Quinn's eye. "Any idea who the father is?"

"No," Quinn replied. "It doesn't matter."

"Well you'll find out soon enough when the baby comes out vanilla or chocolate. No doubt then!"

"Though I prefer a chocolate/vanilla twist, I'll be happy with either flavor." Quinn winked at him.

She was one fine woman. Ty was definitely lucky. Though he wasn't so sure about the sharing part. Ty was openly bi, so maybe he got the best deal, being able to be with a man and a woman. Either way, he wasn't sure how it all worked within their relationship, but it did work. No doubt about that.

Ren moved closer to Ty and slapped his former Boston Bulldogs teammate on the back. "Bro, I hope your swimmers were stronger!"

Logan cleared his throat and caught Ren's attention.

"Congratulations to both of you." Ren offered his hand to Logan, who accepted the invitation and shook it firmly. But he didn't let Quinn's arm go. Logan tended to be possessive like that.

Not that Ren could blame him. Ren had tried to buy his woman a year ago at an auction similar to this one.

"So, I hear you're the victim this time, Renny," Quinn said, squeezing both of her men in closer to her sides.

"Yep. Lucky me. I decided I'm going to kick Dan's ass if he signs me up for any more of these, though." He tilted his head and studied Quinn. "You going to bid on me tonight and save a brother?"

Logan unwound his arm from hers and laid it over her shoulders instead, planting his other hand over her distended belly. A very unmistakable sign of possession.

"She already has her hands full, Renny," Logan told him, his voice a little low and tight.

Logan still had a hard-on over the whole auction thing last year. He needed to move on.

"I remember you trying to buy me at the House to Home Charity that awful night. Hard to believe it was almost a year ago." She frowned. "You ran up the bidding."

"No. I just thought you looked worth every penny. And that dress you wore... Phew." He ran a hand over his forehead, wiping away invisible sweat. "Smokin'."

"I would never fit in that dress now."

"Nothing wrong with having a baby in your belly."

"Really? How'd you like to carry one?" She unconsciously rubbed the small of her back.

"I make them," Ren said. "I don't bake them."

Ren heard a sound from Ty. He saw him struggling not to laugh. Quinn elbowed her lover in the ribs.

"So funny," she said dryly.

Quinn pushed a strand of hair out of her face. Ren was temporarily blinded by the flash of an extremely large blue gem on her left ring finger.

"I remember that sapphire! Nice ring. But it was more beautiful hanging between your breasts."

"It's now my commitment ring."

He raised his eyebrows. "These guys too cheap to buy you diamonds?"

"The sapphire was my late grandmother's. It's one way to remember her." She lifted her hand and shoved it under his nose. "See the two diamonds on both sides of the sapphire?"

Ren captured her hand and studied it. "Can't miss those either."

While he had her hand in his, he pulled her away from her men and escorted her through the building's back door into the hallway. Ty caught the door before it slammed shut behind them. He held the door for his other lover, Logan.

"One is from Logan and one from Ty."

"Cool idea."

Quinn chuckled. "Yes. Very cool."

"So, dog, wanna come to our commitment ceremony?" Ty asked him. "We're only going to have a few people."

"Yes, just a *few*." Quinn said, as if there were going to be way more guests than she wanted. "We'd love for you to come."

Ren didn't miss her eye flick to Logan and back. Ren studied Logan while he asked, "You *all* want me to come?"

Logan, his expression neutral, answered, "Sure. Come. It's going to be a pretty relaxed affair. In fact, bring a date."

The MC's voice came over the loudspeakers. "And now, what you've all been waiting for… The Celebrity Auction!"

Ren winced and cursed. "Gotta go."

"We'll email you an invitation," Quinn called out as he rushed away.

"I'll be there. Just promise there won't be an auction."

As he walked to the stage like a death-row prisoner heading to the electric chair, laughter followed him.

CHAPTER 2

Eve Sanders tapped her freshly manicured nails on the table. *Click. Click. Click. Click.* Until her friend finally pinned her hand onto the table.

"Stop! You're driving me nuts. As well as everyone else at this table!"

She looked at Melody, who was calm and cool while waiting for the latest celebrity on the stage to be "sold." She closed her eyes for a second and swallowed. Hard.

"Please make sure I don't lose."

"If you lose it's because you passed out from your anxiety."

"Then you pick up my paddle and bid for me."

Melody laughed. "You'll be fine." She turned a little in her seat. "Wait, I think he's next."

Eve's heart practically leaped out of her chest. She clenched the auction paddle in her hand even tighter. "Shit."

She should've ordered a drink. Or two.

Melody patted her on the back and laughed.

"Ladies and gentleman, next up is Lawrence 'Long-Arm' Landis, retired quarterback for the World Champion Boston Bulldogs. Look at him, ladies! Isn't he handsome?"

Eve stared at Ren Landis, noticing the expensive cut of his tuxedo, as well as the frown he wore. He was not happy to be on that stage. Not a good sign. *Damn.*

Frown or not, he was a handsome, well-built man. He was tall; the research she'd done said six-foot-two. His skin was a deep, dark tone. She couldn't see his eye color from where she sat, but she'd read they were dark brown.

She'd only seen him once before, which happened to be at a similar charity event, and, unfortunately, it had been from a distance. At that time he had sported short cornrows. Now his hair was trimmed short and tight against his head. She liked it. He wore two large square-cut diamond earrings that sparkled in the overhead lights as he turned and half-heartedly posed at the end of the short stage.

Heat traveled down between her legs, making her shift slightly in her seat. His thighs were thick and muscular under his tuxedo pants and she was sure they had the strength to—

Melody waved a hand in front of her face, breaking her concentration. "Aren't you going to bid?"

With a start, Eve realized the bidding had already begun and the bids were up to $900 already! A lady behind her yelled out $950.

Oh great, while she was spacing out staring at the former NFL player, she almost missed her whole reason for being there.

The female MC yelled into the microphone, "Come on, ladies, you can do better than that! This lean, mean, football machine was the MVP when the Bulldogs won the Super Bowl!"

Ren had to be forcing a smile on his face, because Eve could see it did not reach his eyes. Not even close. Was that a tick in his jaw?

The MC urged him to take off his jacket. He did so reluctantly, his broad shoulders filling out his white dress shirt, while a red cummerbund clung to his trim waist.

Melody's elbow poked at her ribs. "Eve, *bid* before it's over!"

The bid was now at $1050.

Eve caught hold of herself and jerked the auction paddle into the air. She yelled out, "Two thousand dollars!"

The MC echoed her bid. "Wow! That's a jump. A bid of two thousand for Mr. Handsome here!"

A murmur went through the crowd.

The lady somewhere behind her bid against her again. "Twenty-one hundred."

Eve gave a determined smile and lifted her paddle again. "Twenty-five hundred."

Melody leaned over to her and whispered, "What's your max bid, Eve?"

Eve ignored her.

Melody knocked her elbow into her ribs once again. Melody was no longer whispering. "Eve! What's your max bid?"

Eve finally murmured, "Whatever wins him."

"What?"

The lady behind her bid again, yelling out, "Twenty-six hundred."

Eve wanted to turn around and give the other bidder the stink eye, but instead she pursed her lips and let out a ragged breath. She wasn't going to play this game anymore. She came here to win Ren Landis and, damn it, she was going to win him. No matter what.

She stood up without her paddle and said, "Five thousand."

This time it wasn't only murmurs. Eve heard a couple gasps, a "You go, girl," as well as some wild clapping from the corner behind her. She turned to look at the loud clapper and saw Quinn Preston, flanked by her two lovers, at the back corner table.

The other bidder said with disgust in her voice, "You can have him."

The MC repeated her bid a few times, waiting for someone to yell out another bid. Eve closed her eyes, waiting to hear the next bid. The MC kept prodding the audience, trying to get anyone to bid a little higher. Thankfully, no one did.

Finally, the MC yelled out, "SOLD! Five thousand dollars to bidder number ninety-eight!"

Still standing, Eve opened her eyes and looked across the tables to the stage. Her gaze met Ren's. His eyebrows were raised at her and she gave him a shaky smile. He responded to her with a shake of his head and a smile of his own. There was something in that smile, though, that caught Eve off guard, but she couldn't place it.

She sank into her chair. She might have bitten off more than she could chew.

He turned on his heels and strode off the stage, disappearing through the curtain.

"Damn, Eve. Five thousand dollars. I know you wanted him at any cost, but damn! I'm not sure why you wanted him that badly..."

Eve didn't want to have to lie to her friend, so before she answered she thought carefully. As she struggled to find the right answer that wouldn't embarrass her, the stage curtain opened again and the next "celebrity date" sauntered out. To say he was sauntering was an understatement. There was an actual sway to the man's hips, enough to catch Eve's eye. A smile crossed her face. Now with one win under her belt, her confidence had ratcheted up a few notches.

"Are you ready to go settle up?" Melody asked her.

Without even turning her head, Eve asked, "You're not bidding at all tonight?"

"No. I can't afford most of these dates. So I'm ready to go if you are."

Eve pursed her lips and watched the man currently on the stage. He was enjoying the spotlight. "I'm not ready."

"Uh, okay. I guess it doesn't hurt to look at a little more eye candy."

The MC introduced the broad-shouldered man currently on the stage. "Ladies, ladies, ladies and gentlemen, here's another handsome face for you. And the rest of him isn't bad either! And what do you know? A former teammate of the last hunka-hunka-burning love!"

He wasn't quite as tall as Ren. But he was close. She'd guess around six feet or so.

"Cole Dixon is the former NFL running back that also helped the Bulldogs bring home the Super Bowl Championship. I hear he's got some great moves!"

He flashed the audience a sparkling white smile, which contrasted with his deep tan, one only achieved when you spent a lot of time outdoors. He strutted out to the end of the stage, then stopped, his legs spread and his arms crossed, dripping attitude. His tux tightened over his shoulders with the move, giving all the ladies a hint of how broad his shoulders really were. She remembered seeing lots of pictures of Cole Dixon when she was researching Ren. They were close friends and got their photos taken together a lot by the paparazzi. She couldn't quite see his green eyes from where she was, but in the pictures his eyes had been stunning.

"So, ladies, who wants to bid first?"

He didn't look uncomfortable on stage as Long-Arm Landis had. She wondered what Cole's nickname was or if he even had one.

Melody leaned over and said softly, "He's hot."

Eve pushed her chair back and said, "Yes. He is." She stood, forgetting about her auction paddle. She tried to say "Five thousand," but her voice cracked, and she tried again, louder this time. "Five thousand!"

Melody yanked at her arm. "Eve! What are you doing?"

Without a glance to her friend, she answered, "Bidding." She met Cole's eyes on stage and murmured, "No, not bidding. Winning."

She heard her competition behind her curse and say, "I didn't even get a chance before she outbid me!"

The MC was staring at her, almost as if she was waiting for Eve to cancel her bid, to say she made a mistake. "Ma'am, you already won the last date for five thousand dollars."

Eve lifted her chin a little, her eyes never leaving Cole's face.

"Yes, and I want this one, too." Her answer was met by a few chuckles throughout the crowd.

Cole fought to keep his flashy smile in place, but he was clearly struggling with it.

"Well, okay then. Any other bidders? Highest bid is five thousand. Five thousand. Five thousand. Anyone? Fifty-one hundred? Fifty-one hundred? No? No one? Then five thousand dollars it is. Going once. Going twice. SOLD! Five thousand dollars from bidder ninety-eight." The MC stood frozen with the microphone in her hand. Then Eve could see her mentally shake herself back into action. "Um, okay then. Thank you, Mr. Dixon."

Cole Dixon didn't move a muscle. He stood legs apart, arms still crossed over his chest. He simply stared at Eve.

She swallowed and sat down.

Cole licked his lips and his flashy smile was back.

The MC covered her mic and said "Mr. Dixon, you can leave the stage now. Thank you." It was still loud enough that Eve could hear. Cole remained where he stood. Then he began to step forward as if he was going to leap off the front of the stage. But the MC caught his arm and said, "Thank you, Mr. Dixon, please go back that way." She gestured toward the back of the stage and the curtain.

With a tilt of his head, he blew Eve a kiss before turning and walking away.

No. *Now* she may have bitten off more than she could chew.

CHAPTER 3

Right after Eve had won Cole, Melody had pulled her from her seat and dragged her over to settle her bill. She wasn't going to allow Eve to spend any more money on any more men. That was okay with Eve. She'd accomplished what she intended. She had felt a quiet calm while she was writing the $10,000 check. Or so she tried to tell herself. It ended up being a quiet calm before the storm.

Did she really "buy" two men for nefarious reasons? She fought back the nervous laughter wanting to bubble up during their car ride home. No, she hadn't "bought" two men, she'd bought two dates. Dates. That was all it was. And when it hit her how much she'd spent, she told herself it went to a good cause. *Sure.*

Now two days later, she stared at the business card sitting on her kitchen table like a beacon. The business card belonged to the men's sports agent, Daniel Osbourne. Since she had not seen either man after the auction, she had been given the agent's card instead, with his contact information. This Dan guy was supposed to set up the dates. She had fought the urge to call him the next day, but she didn't want to appear too eager. Plus, she was still gathering her nerves. But nerves or not, she was anxious to get the ball rolling. Or balls, she thought, and a little nervous giggle escaped her.

She covered her mouth with her hand, horrified. That was *so* not like her.

As she lifted her cell phone, it rang, startling her. The phone almost slipped from her shaky fingers, but she caught it before it fell to the tile floor. The number of the caller came up as "blocked."

She never answered unknown numbers. She put it on the table as if the person calling might see her holding the phone and ignoring their call. She was being silly. As the ringtone finally quieted, she sighed in relief. Why was she so on edge?

Oh, it was because she was about to call this agent about *the dates.*

Was she having second thoughts?

No. She would not chicken out. No way. No how. *Keep telling yourself that.*

She jumped as her phone rang again. *Blocked number.*

Who blocks their damn number? And then expects people to actually answer it!

She slid her finger across the screen. "Hello?"

A male voice said, "Oh, hey. I didn't think you'd pick up. I was going to leave a message this time."

"Who is this?"

A deep chuckle filled her ear. "You don't recognize my voice?"

"Should I?" Should she know who this was?

"Damn! I'm wounded."

"Do you have the wrong number?"

"I sure hope not."

Wait. This couldn't be—

She pulled out one of the wooden chairs, her hand shaky from adrenaline.

"It's Ren."

"Ren," Eve repeated slowly.

"Wow. You're killing me here. Yeah, you know—Ren Landis? I'm the guy you paid five big ones to go on a date with? Remember him?"

Eve sank down onto the kitchen chair, crushing the business card in her fist. "Oh, Ren. Yes. I'm sorry." She swallowed hard. "I was about to call your agent. I wasn't expecting—"

"Aaaah, I'm just messing with you. I wanted to discuss the date. I had an idea and I wanted to run it past you."

"Oh really? I wasn't sure who got to choose what the date included." Eve heard him snort. She cursed under her breath. "I mean, where we'd go. Or whatever." She bounced her fist off her forehead a couple times. She needed to get it together.

"Well, I usually let the lady make the decision, but that's why I'm calling. I didn't want to go through Dan. I wanted to run this by you first."

Usually? How many times has he done this? "Shoot."

"I've got a buddy who's having a get-together next Saturday night. I thought maybe you could go with me as a date. That's unless you had something else planned…"

"No. I… I actually hadn't thought about what we'd do. I guess that would be okay. He wouldn't mind me coming?"

"No. I was told to bring a date. There's only one little catch."

"What's that?"

"It's a commitment ceremony."

"What do you mean? I mean, I know what a commitment ceremony is, but why would that be a 'little catch'?"

The phone went silent for a moment. On the other end, Ren took a deep breath. "I'll just come out and say it. It's my former teammate Ty White. He and his…lovers…partners…uh, are getting committed to each other…since I guess three adults can't marry each other legally. I guess… I don't know."

Eve perked up. Maybe she should put poor Ren out of his misery. But her head was spinning too fast to process what he was saying. "Wait. Wait! Are you talking about Quinn Preston and her two boyfriends?"

The surprise was clear in Ren's voice. "Yes, you know her?"

"Yes, I've actually met her before. I met her a while back." In fact, it was the first time Eve had seen Ren Landis. It was at the House to Home Charity event that Quinn's mother had organized. A date with Quinn had been auctioned off. Eve had watched the whole bidding war between Quinn's boyfriend Logan and Ren. She'd never forget it. That's when she noticed Ren and she hadn't gotten him out of her mind ever since. It was one reason she, since she sat on the charity's board, had suggested Ren, and later Cole, to be part of the auction that was held the other night.

Watching Quinn with her two men by her side had piqued her curiosity about the idea of being able to love and enjoy more than one man at a time. She hadn't even known where to begin to explore something like that for her own life. And now, because of her interest in Ren, the opportunity to be around Quinn and possibly even to be able to ask her questions, just fell in her lap. She hadn't expected this when she had forked out the five grand for the date with Ren. This was a completely unexpected bonus.

"I would love to go. I've been meaning to contact Quinn anyway and this would be the perfect opportunity for us to have a little girl talk." At least Eve hoped Quinn would be willing to speak to her. From what she knew about Quinn, she was an open and friendly person. And she was very proud of her men.

"Well, that was too easy."

Eve laughed. "Yes, I would really enjoy going to the ceremony with you. Will it be formal or at a church?"

"No. The email said it'll be at their home. It's casual. Unfortunately, though, it's a couple hours' drive for me. I hope you don't mind the travel."

"No, not at all." Not if it gave Eve the opportunity to pick Quinn's brain. Not to mention spend more time with Ren than she thought she'd get on a typical date.

~

Since it turned out Eve lived almost an hour from Ren, he arranged a driver to pick her up. The car that arrived was a blacked-out town car. It might not have been a stretch limo, but she got to sit in the back and enjoy a glass of champagne during the trip. She never pampered herself like this. She hadn't even had a limo for her wedding.

Eve and her husband had not been rich. They had lived modestly, typical middle class—or what used to be the middle class, which was now part of a dying breed.

But her husband had not become a doctor to be rich. Never to be rich. He truly wanted to help people. He had been a humanist at heart, treating everyone equally, and she had loved that about him. It had been one of his most endearing qualities, one of his greatest attractions. He had even worked for over a year with Doctors Without Borders.

His generosity and his selflessness had made Eve a better person.

And though they lived modestly, he had made sure she would be taken care of if he ever died. He had a few life insurance policies. One she had known about. The others, she hadn't.

Because of that, she now she had money like she'd never dreamed of. But it was not worth the loss of her soulmate.

Never that.

Eve shook her head to clear the cobwebs. She meant this evening to be the start of the next chapter of her life. To be more unpredictable, to live more on the edge. To boldly go after what she wanted. Her husband's death proved life was short, so enjoy it while you can...

The driver pulled off the pavement onto a long stone driveway, dust kicking up from the tires. As they approached the clearing, a beautiful, sprawling log ranch home came into view. Even in the darkness it sparkled like a diamond, all lit up.

The car came to a stop in the circular driveway, and before the driver got out to open her door, someone else beat him to it.

Cole Dixon reached out a hand and she took it gratefully as he assisted her out of the car. He certainly wasn't who she was expecting. As she unfolded herself from the back seat, it was hard to miss the mischievous grin he wore.

Once she got her footing in her heels on the stone driveway, she smoothed down her short dress. Sometimes she wasn't so ladylike getting out of a car in a dress, and wearing high heels didn't help.

She didn't even attempt to hide the surprise in her voice. "Hi."

"Hi," he answered, offering the crook of his arm. She took it, once again grateful for his assistance. "I bet you expected Renny."

She looked out the corner of her eyes at him, but quickly returned her attention to where she walked until they reached the smooth surface at the foot of the steps that led up to the huge wraparound porch. She paused. "Yes. This was supposed to be his date night."

He lowered his arm and grabbed her hand before she could move away. Raising her arm above her head, he slowly spun her around like a ballerina in a music box. He let out a low whistle. "Very nice!"

She was *not* going to blush. No she wasn't!

She had worn one of her favorite little black dresses that hung in her closet. This one fell about mid-thigh, and the front of the dress had a diamond cutout, so a tempting, but not indecent, amount of cleavage showed. Sexy, but demure enough to leave something to the imagination. The neckline circled the base of her throat, leaving her shoulders bare. The dress hugged her curves like a lover's hand. The diamond cutout was mirrored on the back of the dress. With her hair pulled up, a few loose tendrils fell down her back to tickle the exposed skin showing through the cutout.

As he finished turning her she came back to face him. The heat in his eyes was unmistakable. And suddenly she knew she had made the right decision to bid on Cole. He exuded lust and sex, but also playfulness. And that discovery made her shiver enough for goosebumps to cover her body. Her nipples pebbled under the dark fabric of the dress and the flick of Cole's eyes showed he hadn't missed her reaction either.

"Cole! You gonna bogart my date all night?"

Eve turned her head to watch the literally tall, dark, and handsome man walk down the steps to meet them.

Cole murmured, "I just might," his gaze never leaving Eve's figure.

"You should've brought your own date, fool."

Eve asked Cole, "You came by yourself?"

"I came with Renny. But if I were him, I would've picked you up instead of me."

As Ren reached the base of the wide steps, he nudged Cole out of the way with his shoulder. "But it's not your date, and you didn't, so go away now." He stepped in front of Eve. "Excuse his lame ass. You look beautiful, and thank you for coming."

She tilted her head. "Thank you for asking."

"Well, I couldn't have Cole as my date all night. He was always good at handling my balls, but..."

She laughed and took his arm when he offered it. He started to escort her up the steps but paused. "Cole, you go first. Otherwise, you'll be watching her ass the whole way up." He leaned into Eve and whispered, loud enough for Cole to hear, "Not that I'd blame him."

"Damn, you can't even throw a brother a bone," Cole griped.

Instead, Eve got to appreciate Cole's muscular ass moving under his slacks as he ran up the steps and into the house. She had to admit the view was spectacular.

As Ren escorted her up the steps to the front door, he said, "You didn't have to dress up, but I'm not complaining. That dress is perfect on you."

"Thanks." Maybe she was dressed a little too formal for what he said was a casual affair, but neither man was a slouch when it came to dressing. Both had on collared dress shirts as well as slacks. Eve hadn't missed the pull of fabric over Ren's heavily muscled thighs either as he had walked up the steps. His body screamed power.

The distraction caused her to stumble a bit, but Ren saved her as he tightened his grip on her arm. "You okay?"

"Perfect."

He led her up the final steps and into the house. As they stepped into a large open room with a two-story ceiling, she was impressed. The house was the right combination of rustic and classy. People swirled around the room socializing, talking, and laughing. She caught a glimpse of Cole speaking to Logan Reed in one corner, while Ty White stood next to Quinn at a table packed with hors d'oeuvres. Ty was patiently holding a plate for Quinn as she filled it up. He had a hand on the small of her back, rubbing it as she moved along the table.

Ren steered her in their direction. "Hungry?"

Eve shook her head. "Not yet. Maybe later."

Ren greeted Quinn and Ty. Quinn was busy putting food in her mouth as well as on the plate. Actually Eve thought most of the hors d'oeuvres never saw the plate.

Ty warned, "Never get in between food and a pregnant woman."

Quinn laughed and said, "I feel as though I'm feeding an army." She turned to face Eve. "I'm glad to see that Renny brought a date!"

"She's the one who paid all that money for me the other night."

Quinn made an *O* with her mouth and Ty looked at her a little closer. He asked, "Why would you do that?"

Eve raised her bare shoulders slightly and laughed. "You don't think he's worth it?"

Ty looked at her with a serious face. "No, he's definitely not worth it."

Ren fake punched Ty's gut. "Bullshit. I'm worth every penny."

Quinn snorted. "You better make it worth her while," she said to Ren. To Eve she shrugged and said, "I don't get it. But to each his own. Sorry that I didn't recognize you as being the winning bidder, but we were sitting in the back."

"And she was too busy stuffing her face and protecting her plate of food like a starving cheetah to pay much attention," Ty joked. He got an eye roll from Quinn as a response.

"What time is the ceremony?" It seemed Ren wanted to change the subject and Eve was fine with that. She wasn't in the mood to field questions about why she not only spent the large sum of money on a single date, but bid on two men. She wanted to keep that information to herself at this point.

Quinn looked at Ty's watch. "Shit. Soon. I need to eat first!"

Ty rolled his eyes at her this time. "You've *been* eating!"

Ren put his palms out in front of him. "Ooo. Never piss off a pregnant woman."

Eve sidled up to Quinn before she belted Ty. "Quinn, do you mind taking a few minutes later to speak with me. I have some questions for you."

Quinn's eyebrows knitted. "Sure. Is it about business concerning House to Home?"

Eve stepped between the men, blocking their view of her face. She nodded her head, but at the same time she mouthed *no*.

"Uh. Sure." Quinn opened her mouth to say something else, but jerked in pain. "Damn, this kid's going to be an NFL kicker." She rubbed her belly with her food-free hand.

Ty stepped around Eve to place a hand along Quinn's belly, feeling for kicks. "That's my boy! Future NFL star."

Eve studied the loving couple as Ty escorted Quinn away.

The look of pride on the man's face was unmistakable—even if he wasn't sure who the biological father of Quinn's baby was. It seemed he couldn't care less, and Eve hoped that attitude continued once the baby was born. She wondered if it was truly possible that two men could be fathers to one baby and not have any issues with it. She supposed if it was possible, those three would be able to achieve it. She had read online that they already knew it was a boy and would name him Preston Reed White, the perfect combination of all their last names.

"Hello? Are you in there?"

Eve realized she had been caught up in her own thoughts, and turned to the handsome man next to her. "Sorry."

"Where did you go?"

She shook her head. "They have a beautiful home. Do they all sleep in the same bedroom?"

"That's where you went? Damn! I like a woman who thinks about the important stuff." He laughed at his own teasing. "But yes, Ty told me once that they did."

"So you had asked too?"

"Of course I did! I'm only human." He wiggled his eyebrows at her, giving her a broad smile. He had a beautiful smile and it was infectious. "Do you want to go sneak a peek?"

Heat filled Eve's cheeks. "No! I don't want to intrude on their privacy."

Ren waved a hand at her, like it was no big deal. "Fine. Let's go out and find a seat. Seems like everyone's starting to head that direction."

They followed the stream of people out onto the back deck and down steps to the backyard. There seemed to be no end to the well-tended grass, as the backyard was bordered by fields of turf. It was common knowledge the three of them ran a very successful sod business and some of their biggest customers were football stadiums—high school, college, and even professional.

Plenty of decorated folding chairs were set up, all facing a beautiful trellis archway, covered in ivy, flowers, and twinkling little white lights. It was very romantic, and Eve felt a pang of longing. She wanted a relationship as solid and loving as this trio had.

Ren found them seats and before she was even settled in hers, Cole came from her right to sit down beside her.

"Hi."

She looked at him and returned his smile. "Hi." He was an extremely beautiful man. It was hard to look at him and not smile. She had to adjust a bit in her chair as both men's broad shoulders took up some of her personal space. Not that she was complaining. Who in their right mind would complain about being sandwiched between two such masculine men?

Her nostrils flared, catching Ren's delicious scent as he leaned over her to address his friend. He definitely smelled good enough to eat. "You are going to have to wait your turn, Dix."

"Oh, this is your official date tonight?" he teased Ren. "Are you sure?" Cole winked at her.

She fought back a giggle over the playful competition between the two. "You better not think that this is considered your date as well," she warned Cole.

"Oh, believe me, I don't. Tonight's only a bonus for me. I look forward to our date. I promise it'll be more private."

Ren gave him a sharp glance and it looked as though he was going to respond to the other man, but the violinist started to play and he settled back in his chair.

By the end of the short and sweet service, none of the three involved in the commitment ceremony had dry eyes. But when Quinn and her men turned to face the small audience, despite the tears, they all wore larger-than-life smiles and appeared extremely happy. Very content.

They had committed themselves to each other for the rest of their lives. They might never be able to legally marry each other as a threesome, but it was close enough. They had ended up exchanging infinity rings instead of plain wedding bands, and Eve thought it was a perfect touch.

The rest of the evening included a bonfire and music, lots of food, and celebrating. Ren was a complete gentleman...for the most part.

During the ceremony, he kept touching Eve. Her arm, her knee, her elbow. Touches that could be considered gentlemanly, but lingered a tad longer than was necessary. Each brush of his fingers invoked a quick shiver, or goosebumps, or even a tightening of her nipples.

He knew exactly was he was doing to her. And she caught him wearing a Cheshire cat smile several times.

He placed a hand on her elbow as he now guided her around, saying hello to other guests, and again to steer her away when Cole came close.

"Are you normally this hands-on with your auction dates?"

He chuckled and shook his head, the diamond studs in his ears reflecting the lantern lights strung around the immense deck at the back of the house. "No. Usually I'm the one fighting the women off. They feel as though they paid for me so they get to do what they want. You seem to be…different."

Maybe not so different after all. If he only knew what she was thinking, what she was planning. Maybe he might end up fighting her off also.

"Cole told me you bought him that night, too."

Bought. It sounded just…wrong.

"I was the highest bidder, you mean," she corrected him.

"Bought. Highest bidder. Same shit. Prettier words." He studied her for a moment. "Were you just feeling generous that night or—"

"Maybe I'm merely lonely."

"I doubt that."

Eve shrugged in response, but was relieved he didn't push her for answers.

He put a hand on her back. The width of his hand practically spanned the small of her back. Strong, big hands were needed to hold and throw a football with accuracy. She caught herself looking down at his shoes.

So did he. "Size thirteen."

She closed her eyes and at least had the decency to blush before meeting his gaze. "I wasn't…"

He gave her a broad smile. "Oh yes, you were."

He led her toward the other side of the deck, his hand firmly steering her toward the small bar set up in a corner.

"Let me buy you a drink."

"It's not a cash bar."

"Humor me. What do you want?"

"An extra dirty martini." She added a quick, "Please."

"You hear that?" He asked the bartender, a fresh-faced young man who didn't look much older than twenty-one. "She'd like a martini. But she likes hers *extra dirty*."

"Yes, sir, Mr. Landis. And for you?"

"Whatever you have on tap."

Once they had their drinks in hand, they wandered away to a quieter corner.

"So, are you a lady's man?"

He glanced over to the crowd, scanning it, before his gaze landed back on her. He tilted his head slightly as if to read her mind. He broke eye contact and stared over her shoulder once again. She turned slightly to look; she saw nothing out of the ordinary. "Oh, I like the ladies." He took a sip of his beer. "But they tend to not like me after a while."

"I've seen some of the gossip magazines. Hard to miss them at all the grocery store checkouts. They tend to be a bit 'in your face.'"

"Don't believe everything you read."

Eve murmured, "That's good to hear." She didn't want to admit she'd bought one—or two—in the past when he'd been on the cover. Usually with a gorgeous model on his arm. Or at a club. Or in one of his expensive cars.

She thought of all the online research she had done on him. Anything they could dig up on him, they did. Paternity tests. Punching a photographer. Ditching a famous date at a busy night club.

"This is supposed to be a date, not an exposé. Are you a reporter?"

"Me?" She laughed. "Oh no. I'm a pretty private person, so I tend to respect other people's privacy as well."

"Then why the interest?"

Eve lifted a shoulder. "Simply getting to know you."

"Why? You get one date." He looked harder at her, as if he was trying to peel away her layers to get to the truth. "After tonight, we'll go our separate ways."

She didn't answer him. She didn't know what to say, or even how to say it if she did.

"Look, I'm not looking for anything long term. That's usually why I end up in the gossip columns."

"Me neither. I was married for over ten years."

"*Was.* Divorced?"

She looked away. It was her turn to be fascinated by something she couldn't see. "I don't want to talk about it," she said, absently.

"Got it."

She noticed him looking at her left hand. She didn't hide the fact she still wore her diamond wedding band. He didn't ask about it, though. It brought him up a notch with her. She liked people who respected other people's privacy, as she did. She was sure he got tired of being constantly in the public eye, under scrutiny. Especially since some of the reported stories were false. Or exaggerated.

She spotted Quinn heading into the house through the sliding glass doors.

"Sorry, do you mind if I go talk to Quinn for a couple minutes? I have some business to talk to her about."

He didn't answer her at first, and she didn't want to be rude, but she was anxious to speak with Quinn.

He finally said, "No, go ahead. I'm on your dime."

Eve didn't know him well enough to figure out if he wasn't happy about it and merely being shitty, or he truly didn't mind. Either way, he was right. He was on her dime. "I promise I won't be long."

As she turned, he caught her hand and lifted it to his lips. He kissed the back of her left hand, right above her wedding ring, before letting her go. "I'll be waiting."

She didn't remember anyone ever kissing the back of her hand before, and had never expected such tenderness from a football player. She remembered the jocks from high school and college, and thought they had all acted like meatheads. Maybe it had to do with their age. Either way, she found it curious. She shook her head and followed Quinn into the house.

As Ren watched her walk away, he couldn't help but watch those hips move in a dress that hugged her luscious curves. Her hips were what his grandmamma used to call "baby-making hips." She was not what he would call skinny, impossible with all those curves. Her hips weren't fat, but just soft enough to give him something to hold on to.

He judged her to be a few years younger than him, maybe thirty or so. She appeared classy, but not overly sophisticated. Definitely not stuck up.

She was maybe about a foot shorter than his six-foot-two. But those curves. They were perfect for her stature. *Damn.*

And her eyes, lined with thick lashes, were gold one minute, green the next, rimmed in a dark brown. Those eyes kept him guessing. If he wasn't careful, he could get lost in them.

Her breasts were full. Nothing unnatural about them as her luscious cleavage was revealed through the diamond cutout of her dress. *Luscious.* Luscious hips. Luscious breasts. The word described her to a T.

He could not stand fake anything on a woman, be it nails, tits, ass, eyelashes, or hair. He wanted a woman who was the old phrase, WYSIWYG. What you see is what you get. No surprises.

Her hair was long. He had noticed the length at the auction where she wore it down, and it fell to her mid-back. Tonight, she had it pulled up, with a few sexy reddish blonde tendrils falling down around her shoulders.

Her skin was like ivory, and with that color hair, he bet under her makeup was a sprinkle of freckles over her nose. With her hair in a ponytail and no makeup, she would look like the all-American "girl next door."

He could live with that.

With her hair up as it was tonight, she would only need a pair of glasses and a pencil tucked behind her ear to look like a naughty librarian, exuding sex. Though none of the librarians he knew as a kid ever looked like that. But if she was one, he'd be making a racket in her quiet library so she'd be forced to chide him. Maybe even give him some well-deserved punishment.

His cock twitched. He had a damn chubby because of that little fantasy. *Double damn!*

After talking to her for most of the evening and listening to her talk with other guests, he concluded she was smart. Extremely. She could hold her own in any conversation she was included in.

Looks, body, *and* a brain. Now all she had to be was a little wildcat in bed and she'd be perfect.

Every woman who tried to hook claws in Ren in the past had been missing at least one of his requirements. Maybe that made him sound like an ass. He had been called that plenty of times, and much worse. But, hell, a woman had to "do it" for him to be more than simply a fuck. He had to be able to spend time with the woman, actually be able to have a worthwhile conversation with her. He didn't want to feel like he was only a trophy or a wallet to them, or for them to be eye candy on his arm. Those types were a dime a dozen. He wanted a woman with substance.

Maybe he was too picky. Maybe that's why he had never been in a relationship for any length of time.

They would have bits and pieces of what he was looking for, but never the complete package.

And Eve had a very nice package.

The night wasn't even over yet, and, surprisingly, he already knew he had to see her again. Even though he had already made clear it would only be one date.

My bad.

～

It was no surprise when Eve found Quinn at the buffet table.

Quinn laughed. "You caught me grazing again. I never thought I could eat this much."

"Well you *are* eating for a future NFL star, right?"

Quinn laughed again. "So Ty thinks. And thank you for not making me feel so guilty." She sobered and looked at Eve seriously. "You wanted to talk to me?"

"Yes, if you don't mind."

"By the way you asked earlier, I assume it's nothing you want Renny to know about? That means it should be in private?"

"Yes. Again, only if you don't mind."

"Can I get you to massage my feet while we talk?"

Eve opened her mouth, but no sound escaped.

Quinn laughed again and patted Eve on the arm. "Eve, I'm kidding. But seriously though, I wouldn't complain if the boys hired me a full-time massage therapist. If one of those men had to carry this kid, you had better believe we'd have at least one masseuse on staff." She finished filling a small plate with veggies and dip. "Follow me."

Eve did. They ended up in the master bedroom, sitting on the enormous bed.

Quinn placed the plate down between them. "I have no idea what this is about, so just shoot."

Eve didn't know how to start. "I..." She blushed, then cursed herself.

"I guess this doesn't have anything to do with the charity, otherwise you wouldn't be turning bright red. I don't know you well enough to know your personal life, so does this have anything to do with me?"

"How does it work for you?"

Quinn blinked. "How does what work for me?"

Eve swept a hand toward the bed they were sitting on. "All this. You. The guys."

"You mean sex?"

The heat in Eve's cheeks flamed again. "No, sorry. I meant the relationship. The three of you."

Quinn froze, her hand paused halfway to her mouth with a baby carrot loaded with dip.

Eve quickly followed with, "I'm sorry if that's too personal of a question for you. But I'm envious of what you have. I think it works for you three. I don't know how it does, but it seems as though it does."

She put the carrot back on the plate and shifted to face Eve more directly. Her eyes narrowed. "Why do you care how it works for us?"

"I'm sorry if you think this is strange. I'm not trying to dig into your personal lives, or even your sex life. Remember when I met you at the—"

"Yes, yes! At the House to Home Monte Carlo night my mother hosted at the country club. I almost forgot that was where I first met you!"

"Yes. You really caught my attention there. All of you."

Quinn chuckled and put a hand to her belly. "Yeah. We caught a lot of people's attention. It wasn't like we were subtle."

Eve smiled. "It was hard to miss, but you three weren't the only people I noticed."

Quinn made an *O* with her lips. "Renny?"

"Yes."

"He's not very subtle either. He certainly catches the women's eyes."

"Yes, he's very handsome."

"But he doesn't have a good track record with women."

"I know." She hesitated, but figured it was now or never. "How well do you know Cole?"

"Not as well as Renny, but— Wait." Quinn's eyebrows knitted together. "You don't want to ask me about Renny?"

Eve looked down at her hands. She was wringing them. She pulled them apart and tried to lay them calmly on her thighs.

She couldn't look at Quinn when she said, "Actually, I want to ask you about both...sort of."

Quinn hesitated and from the corner of her eye, Eve could see Quinn tilting her head and studying her. She finally said, "Both." It wasn't a question. "I think I'm starting to figure out where you're going with this."

Good. Because I'm not sure I am. She knew what she wanted, but she wasn't sure how to go about it. If talking with Quinn could spark some kind of idea...

"Are you... Do you think..." Quinn shook her head and started again. "Are you planning on trying a threesome with Cole and Renny?"

"Well, I mean not just sex; sex is usually the easy part. I meant a relationship with both of them. Though from what I know about Renny, the sex may not be the easy part. At least with another man involved. Even if it *is* Cole."

Quinn looked shocked. "Damn, girl, you have some *cajones*. But I don't blame you." She shook her head, and the shock quickly changed to approval. "No, I definitely don't blame you. Wait. Do they even know?"

"No. That's why I wanted to talk to you and ask you how this all worked between you and Ty and Logan."

"It works very well. *Now*. However, there was a little jealousy in the beginning. Not from me though."

"Who?"

"Ty. You have to understand that I started out as the third wheel. Logan and Ty were already lovers and living together. And theirs wasn't a new relationship. They were already bonded. And then one night Logan brought me home. That's a long story..." She absently rubbed her distended belly. "But, anyway, never in my wildest dreams would I have ever thought I'd be committed to two men at the same time. Hell, even pregnant! I love them both so much." She finally shoved the baby carrot into her mouth and chewed thoughtfully. "Oh, boy… I don't know if what you want will work. No one's currently in a relationship. It's going to be all new and there will be some growing pains. Hell, probably a lot of growing pains. It may be a complete failure. It would be a shame if something like this tore Cole and Renny's friendship apart." She continued to stare off while thinking.

Eve could see the wheels turning in her head and didn't want to interrupt.

"Cole may be easy. He's an extremely sexual being, from what I know about him. He loves the human body and sex. If it's someone who 'does it' for him, he doesn't care whether it's a man or a woman, at least from what I've seen and heard. He may be more open-minded to try what you're asking." She paused and again thought for a moment. "Renny… Renny, on the other hand…" She blew out a breath. "Renny I'm not so sure about. He loves women. And unfortunately, the women love him and usually the wrong ones. I don't know of any relationship that he's been in that's been successful or lasted any length of time. He just… I don't know you very well, but from the little that I know, I suspect you may be good for him. You seem to have your head screwed on straight. Even though I think you may have to be a little crazy to try this."

Eve only nodded her head, still unwilling to interrupt Quinn. Whatever wisdom the other woman had, she wanted it.

"Let me say this. Polyamory isn't for everybody. It takes work. A lot. And you are starting from nothing. The only thing that exists is the boys' friendship. If you can use that to build upon, more power to you. The dynamics may be a bit different than ours. I'm pretty sure Renny is very heterosexual."

Quinn immediately stopped talking when Logan stepped into the room. "What are you two talking so seriously about? This is supposed to be a celebration. Can I steal her away?"

"Of course." Eve was disappointed that Quinn's out-loud thinking had been interrupted, but Logan was right, this was a night for celebrating their relationship, and she didn't want to be selfish or rude.

"Sorry," Quinn apologized. "We can always talk later."

Logan helped Quinn up off the bed, one hand caressing her belly, the other holding her by the shoulder to steady her.

Ty suddenly appeared, too. His arm reached around her extended waist, assisting Quinn to waddle across the room. Eve didn't miss the smiles the three of them gave each other. A secret thought shared.

Hard to believe that two men and one woman could achieve such bliss. Too many couples struggled in relationships. If the rate of failed marriages was so high, why did she think that a threesome could make it in a successful relationship?

She was getting ahead of herself. She hardly knew either man. She only knew *about* them; she didn't *know* them.

She had a lot of discovery to do. And quick.

Well, the night was young, right?

CHAPTER 4

The gathering finally came to a close shortly after midnight, when Quinn could no longer contain her yawns. She had lost her shoes hours before, her swollen feet unable to be contained anymore. Finally, after she disappeared, everyone started to say their goodbyes and wander out to their vehicles.

Ren decided that instead of separate cars he would use his rented limo to drop both Cole and Eve off. In that order too, since Cole was closer. His wasn't the typical limo that had come to Eve's mind. It was an extended Cadillac Escalade.

The driver opened the doors for them, but it was Ren that helped her step up into the high vehicle. She did it with as little grace as she had getting out of the town car earlier in the evening.

Eve felt her dress working its way up her thighs as she climbed into the vehicle and slid onto one of the overstuffed soft leather seats. Ren followed behind her and sat directly across from her, while Cole entered from the other side and plopped himself beside her, only a center console separating them.

She wiggled deeper into her seat with a sigh, and when she was settled, she realized Ren's eyes had dropped below her dress's hemline. She followed his gaze and noticed the lacy tops of her stockings peeking out. No, they weren't peeking out—her dress had worked its way up her legs much too high. The garterless stockings were clearly on display. Ren stared for a long second; then he slowly raised his eyes to meet hers. A wicked grin crossed his face, causing heat to rise into her cheeks.

Her first instinct was to pull her dress down, like a respectable lady should. But she fought it; she was tired of being a lady, not to mention respectable. She had worn this particular dress and those particular stockings because they made her feel sexy. And, damn it, she was going to enjoy the reaction she was getting.

Cole's eyes drew to where Ren's were staring, and he let out a long, low whistle. "Damn."

Ignoring him, she ran her hand over the smooth leather of the seat. "Very nice."

"I agree," Cole echoed her. But she doubted he was talking about the SUV.

"A little ostentatious for my taste," Ren murmured. "But I took what was available."

Big word for a football player, but in truth, it hadn't surprised her. Throughout the evening Eve had been impressed with Ren's intelligence. No matter what the subject, or who he was talking to, he always kept up with the conversation. In fact, it was never him that brought up sports, but others would. She was pleased he was not only extremely handsome, but extremely intelligent and well-rounded, too.

Cole laughed. "Yeah, like your own Escalade isn't *ostentatious*, with those big-assed rims on it and—"

"Let's not talk about vehicles, Dix. You have one helluva collection yourself."

"I can't help it if I have good taste!"

They continued to rib each other good-naturedly until they finally dropped Cole off at what looked like a high-rise apartment complex. But Eve guessed it was more likely condominiums, as a uniformed doorman stood out front.

Cole kissed her on the cheek before sliding out. "I'll call you about our date. Let me give you my digits, so I can call you directly, and you'll know who it is." Eve entered his number into her cell phone while he stood outside the vehicle, leaning in through the open door. He gave her a wink. "Bye."

Eve smiled at him. "Bye." And he slammed the door shut. She watched the sway of his hips as the doorman opened the double glass doors to let him into the building. Before she could let out a sigh, the driver of the Escalade pulled away, breaking her thoughts. Or dirty thoughts, more like it.

"I miss the days of bench seats, where you could slide next to your date and hold her close."

Eve doubted he was old enough to remember bench seats in vehicles, not that it mattered.

"I would love for you to come sit on my lap for the remainder of the ride."

Eve's eyebrows rose, and she tilted her head to look at him. He was straight-faced, so she wasn't quite sure if he was kidding or serious. "Really."

He nodded slightly. "Really." He leaned over to clasp her hand and tug slightly. "You can say no."

She looked down at their clasped hands, his so dark compared to her pale skin. His fingers were long, slender, and well-defined, his nails short and neat. He wore no jewelry on his wrist or fingers. She gripped his hand a little tighter. This was her chance to test the waters with him. She wanted to get to know him better, but not for him to think she was some crazy groupie who was only looking for a notch on her bedpost.

"Maybe I don't want to say no." She moved over to him to settle at an angle on his lap. He placed his arms around her, one hand on her left hip, his other hand along her right thigh. Heat pooled between her legs, and butterflies bounced around in her stomach. His lap was larger than the average man's; he had very thick, muscular thighs. In fact, it would take almost both of her thighs together to equal his one.

"You fit perfectly." His breath tickled the hair along her cheek, and his voice was low and close to her ear.

She shivered at the deep timbre.

"Are you scared?"

She shook her head, but couldn't form any words.

The index finger on his right hand pushed the hem of her dress up, barely enough so he could trace the lace at the top of her stocking. "This is sexy as shit."

She leaned her head back against his shoulder and turned her head a bit to smile at him. But she was too close to his jaw for him to see it. The thumb on his left hand rubbed along her hip as he still traced the top of the stocking with his right.

"Can you feel me?"

She slowly let out a shuddered breath, as the heat and hardness of him unmistakably pressed against her ass.

His index finger turned to his whole hand as he started to stroke her right thigh from under her hemline almost to her knee.

"Have you ever been with a brother before?"

The unexpected question caught her off guard. "No. Does it matter?"

"Not to me, but it may for some people."

"I'm not some people."

A slow smile crossed his face. "No, you are definitely not."

His right hand stroked even higher, until he was skimming his knuckles along her panties. She was damp and warm, inviting him to become even bolder, his hand separating her thighs, giving him room to trace her outer folds through the silky fabric.

She buried her face in his neck and gasped. She shifted her hips to feel his long, hard cock against her as he traced a finger under the line of her panties.

"Can I take these off?"

She wanted to scream "YES!" but instead whispered it shakily into his neck. She planted her mouth against his skin and licked him a second before sinking her teeth into him lightly.

He made a sound similar to a growl, a vibration low in his chest against her.

Ren hooked a finger around the edge of her panties and slowly slid them down her thighs, over her knees until they fell around her ankles. He opened her thighs wider, and pushed her dress until it was above her hips, giving him the access he needed and she wanted. His fingers played along her creases and folds, dipping to caress her clit. She cried out and her hips jerked against his hand. He separated her folds and worked a finger into her tightness. It had been a while for her, so even as wet as she was, she was still tight.

He worked a second finger inside her. He pushed them deep before stilling. Her muscles clamped tightly around him, her breathing heavy. He wrapped one arm around her shoulders to keep her still against his chest. She was desperate for him to caress her nipples, which were pressed hard against her dress. She needed his hands, his mouth on her. But as soon as he moved his long fingers inside her, she forgot all of that. She concentrated on the rhythm he found deep within her. Sounds escaped her as she pressed her face against his neck, her eyelids fluttered closed.

His other hand grasped her chin and he kissed her. Her mouth was open, gasping for breath, but he possessed it anyway. She mewed into his mouth, his tongue tangling with hers. The heat built up low within her and she started to grind against his fingers. His thumb circled her clit, pressing, flicking.

The two fingers inside her curved, finding the spot. The one that always drove her over the edge. Within seconds it did exactly that. She pulled away from his mouth and released a surprising wail. Toes curling in her heels, she clamped around his fingers, as wave after wave of orgasms made her thrash against him. He tightened the arm around her shoulders, trying to still her as he withdrew his fingers. She automatically ground down against his hard cock.

He hissed and held her tighter. "Don't." Her eyes fluttered back open and he had his face turned away, his eyes closed, and his brow furrowed. He was struggling. She moved her hips again, wanting all of him deep inside her. "Don't," he repeated, his voice low and deep, almost growly. "I don't want to embarrass myself in front of you."

Her breathing slowed and she snuggled deeper against him. He blew out a breath and studied her. "Damn. I could take you right here."

In the low light of the interior of the vehicle, she couldn't quite read his eyes, but his expression was no doubt strained.

She reached down to touch him, and in a flash, he captured her wrist, pinning her hand against his chest. "You're trying to play with fire. And I am not prepared."

His hard cock was proof he was ready. But that wasn't what he was talking about. She realized what he was implying. No protection. She did a quick mental inventory of her clutch purse; she didn't have anything with her either. *Damn.*

She looked out of the darkened windows at the surrounding area. She recognized some of the street names under the streetlights. They were getting close to her home anyway. *Double damn.*

She pulled her panties up from around her ankles and wiggled back into them as she shifted back to her seat.

He couldn't keep his eyes off her. But it was mutual.

"Thank you."

He grinned. "My pleasure."

She returned his grin. "No, it was *my* pleasure."

"I would love to do it again sometime."

"Me too."

The SUV came to a sudden stop. She peered out through the darkness. She was home.

"You're very responsive. I like that in a woman."

"You're not selfish when it comes to sex. I like that in a man."

He chuckled, low and deep.

The driver opened the door and the interior light was suddenly blinding. She blinked, trying to clear her vision.

Ren got out first and offered his hand to help her out of the vehicle.

He walked her to the door, which pleased her. He was quite the gentleman.

"Are you always a gentleman?"

He looked down into her face. The smile was gone. With a serious expression, he answered. "No."

She gave him direct eye contact and said, "Good."

He leaned in to give her a soft kiss before drawing back slowly. "Thank you for being my date tonight."

She instinctively reached out to straighten the collar on his shirt. An old habit coming back to the surface. "I should be thanking you."

"I'll call you."

"You don't have to. You were only obligated for one date," she reminded him.

"I want to."

She smiled as she pulled the house keys out of her clutch. "Okay. I look forward to it." She realized he wasn't going to leave until she was safely in the house. She unlocked the door and stepped through the threshold.

"Me too."

His low, sexy voice made her turn to watch him stride away. She closed the door and then leaned against it. As she dropped the clutch to the floor, the solid door at her back held her up. Her heart was beating intensely.

Tonight went way better than she'd expected.

Her instinct had been right about Ren Landis. She'd made the right choice.

She kicked off her shoes and danced her way through the house.

CHAPTER 5

She thought she'd hear from Ren again before Cole, but she was wrong. Cole called her the next day and asked if she minded going to a small club with him that night. So much for the private date Cole hinted at the night before.

At first she thought they had been lucky to get a table toward the front of the stage, but it turned out the reason Cole wanted to hear this band was he had played college football with the drummer. He hadn't seen him in years, so he didn't want to miss the opportunity to support his former classmate/teammate's music.

Cole hadn't given her a lot of details ahead of time, but he picked her up and they made small talk during the drive to the club. It turned out that the Philadelphia-based band, Thorazine, played old-school 90s punk, not music she normally listened to. But it was fast paced and the crowd was fun and energetic. Their table was to the side of the crowd that packed the floor in front of the stage, where the fans were jumping up and down, and even sometimes slamming into each other…on purpose.

The music was loud and so was the crowd. In the end, the music was so deafening that they didn't get to talk much. But between songs, Cole promised her they would get to talk later.

Cole kept her flush with extra dirty martinis, while he nursed a Long Island iced tea. He didn't seem much of a drinker, and she was more than okay with that. She enjoyed a well-made cocktail, but wasn't a big drinker herself. She hadn't had this many martinis in a long time. She made sure to slowly sip them, since as soon as her glass got low, Cole would order her another.

One thing she noticed throughout the evening was the attention that Cole attracted, not only because of his football fame, but because he was *so* beautiful. Women of all ages would sneak peeks at him, circle their table, and some were outright bold enough to slip him their number, or even touch him as they walked by.

At first Eve would hide her smile behind her martini when she noticed their actions, but as the night wore on, she wouldn't hide her smile when she got dirty looks. How lucky was she that she was with such a stunning man? Well, she guessed she had five grand worth of luck. He might not have given her the time of day normally if she hadn't won a date with him at the auction.

But whatever. She got to spend the evening with him and the other catty women did not. And she was going to enjoy every minute. She could lose herself quickly in his amazing green eyes and easy smile.

But Eve was pleased he wasn't merely looks. He had substance. She noticed that the night of the commitment ceremony—the few times Ren would let him even close to her. And she learned more about him simply from the small talk during the drive to the bar.

During a break between sets, his old schoolmate, Dallas Cantland, climbed off the stage to join them. Cole stood up and did the clasp hands, bump shoulders sort of greeting. Dallas had a towel around his neck, and kept wiping the sweat off his smooth bald head. Cole introduced her.

"You're a great drummer!" Eve said, while shaking his hand. While she may not like his genre of music, she recognized the skills of the musicians.

Dallas spun an empty chair around at their table to sit backward on it, leaning against the back of the seat.

Eve could feel him checking her out, or at least eyeing what he could see since she was sitting… It was enough to feel his gaze from her cleavage to the top of her head.

He shot her a big smile. "Wow, smart *and* beautiful." He turned to Cole and elbowed him. "Where did you find her?"

Eve tried not to blush. She didn't like liars, but she hoped Cole ended up stretching the truth a bit. He didn't.

Cole gave him a mouthy smile. "She bought me at an auction."

"What? What? What?" Dallas' eyebrows rose. "No she didn't. You're fucking with me."

Eve placed a hand to her hot face. "No. I didn't *buy* him. I bid on a date with him for charity."

"Same shit," both men said at the same time. They looked at each other in surprise and then laughed.

"Damn, it's been years," Dallas said to Cole.

"I know. Once we were out of college, you got busy with music and me with football."

"Dallas, you didn't want to pursue football?" Eve asked him.

He shook his head. "I was good enough in football to put me through college but wasn't good enough to get drafted, and I was A-okay with that. Being a drummer is the shit and I get to tour all over the country and Canada. You can't beat that."

Eve thought Cole might argue that point. The football star did have a Super Bowl ring and, she assumed, a nice fat bank account. But he didn't mention it, and for that he went up a notch in her eyes.

Dallas turned to her. "Do you like the music?"

She smiled, choosing her words carefully, "It's a lot of fun. I especially liked the last song before the break."

Dallas chuckled quietly, as if he knew it wasn't her type of music and she was only being polite. "There comes a time when you will know and you will see/Accept your place, your life, your vulnerabilities/Look within yourself and you do it on your own…"

Eve looked at him in surprise. "What?"

"Those are the lyrics. The song's title is *The End*."

She shook her head and stood, pushing her chair back. "Dallas, would you like something to drink?"

He shook his head. "I have something on stage, but thanks."

She glanced at Cole. "Excuse me while I head to the ladies' room. It'll give you a few minutes to catch up."

She straightened the skirt she had worn for the evening, and turned to go.

Dallas's words stopped her in her tracks. "What an onion!"

Eve turned back to him and frowned. "I'm sorry?" Maybe he thought she was being rude by excusing herself.

"An onion," Dallas repeated, as if she should know what he meant.

Cole gave her a look and shrugged.

"That ass. It's like an onion, 'cause that thing is going to make me cry."

Cole laughed and Eve finally released her breath. She gave Dallas a big smile and turned to head toward the restrooms. She shook her head with a laugh and made sure she swung her hips more than usual. She could feel their gaze watching her walk away. She was pleased with their reaction, as she wanted Cole hook, line, and sinker…

When she returned to the table, they were wrapping up their conversation, and Dallas stood next to the table. The men bumped fists, and Dallas pulled out her chair for her.

She thought, what a gentleman, until he leaned over to Cole and whispered, "Bang that ass like a screen door in a hurricane!" Only the whisper really wasn't. It was one of those "whispers" loud enough to be heard over the crowd and the background filler music. Not so subtle, and Eve's face filled with heat.

He then leaned down and kissed her on the cheek, and as she

moved to sit in her chair, he swatted her on the ass. She fell into her seat with a thump, surprised, and watched Dallas walk back to the stage, his loud laughter following him.

Cole turned to her and grabbed the hand she had laid on the table. "I'm sorry." He brushed a kiss over her knuckles.

"For what?"

He turned her hand over and rubbed his thumb over her palm. "For Dallas being such a lech."

She gave him a warm smile, and wrapped her fingers around his. "He wasn't. I bet he'd be a lot of fun to hang out with."

"We had a blast in college."

She had no doubt, with Dallas being the character he was. "What was your major?"

"Does it matter? It was only a formality. It was a foot in the door to go pro."

She shrugged slightly. "I'm just curious."

"I'm curious about you, too."

"You're trying to change the subject."

He tilted his head, and it made Eve catch her breath. His green eyes were beautiful. His skin was deeply tanned, like he was outside a lot. She wondered if it was really a tan, or simply a darker skin tone. His career could've easily been modeling instead of sports. In fact, she'd seen quite a few ads with him in it. He was a natural. He had beautiful features, but was still all male.

Eve realized she always thought of him as beautiful, which is certainly not the normal description for a man. But he was and he could pull it off.

"Communications."

"Sorry?"

"That was my major. I thought if my football career came to an early end, that I could be a sportscaster."

"Nothing wrong with that. It's something you can still do now that you're retired at the ripe old age of thirty-four."

He got serious for a moment. "I retired when I was thirty-four.

I'm now almost thirty-six."

"Wow! Ready for the old folk's home," she teased.

"Sometimes my body feels that way."

"Really?"

"Really," he answered her in a serious tone.

Eve wanted to dig deeper into the subject, but the whole band had returned on stage and the music made it impossible for them to finish the conversation.

Cole leaned over the table and yelled into her ear. "You want to get out of here?"

Eve was relieved. She mouthed *Yes* to him, and he offered a hand to help her out of her chair.

His fingers were long and warm as they strongly wrapped around hers. She could hardly make out his words when he yelled, "Let's get outta here."

They didn't say a word until both doors were closed on his old muscle car the valet pulled around. The silence of the closed car was deafening.

Cole finally broke it. "The night's still young yet."

"Yes." The night *was* young with still so much potential.

He placed a hand over hers, which was resting on her thigh. "Where to now?"

"Somewhere quiet?"

His fingers flexed over hers. "Have you ever driven stick?"

She shook her head.

He interlaced his fingers with hers and placed their linked hands over the gear shift. "You don't know what you're missing. All that power within your fingertips." With his hand guiding hers, he shifted the restored classic Camaro into first gear. He let out the clutch and the big block engine roared to life as he pulled away from the club, the tires chirping a bit. He continued to drive through the city with her hand under his on the gear shift. Her hand felt tiny in comparison to his broad palm and long fingers.

She didn't bother to ask where he was headed. She didn't even care. The warm, long fingers intertwined with hers had such promise. She hoped he was just as skilled with them as Ren had been the night before.

That thought made her sit back in the bucket seat. This was what she wanted. What she intended. But could she live with herself for being so open to sex on the first date with two different men? Two men she only had knowledge of because they had lived a very public life?

She had picked them for a reason. They were both men who had played the field. And she wasn't thinking about football. Both had been sexually active with women, and in Cole's case, also with men, but didn't take relationships seriously. She figured they'd be more open-minded to what she would propose. If they agreed, she hoped it would eventually work out to be long-term but reminded herself not to be disappointed if it didn't. Either way, she wanted to explore her sexuality, wanted to explore something new. Both men seemed to be secure enough in their sexuality, from what she could see.

He worked his way through the city with skill. It was clear he knew it well, and it wasn't long before he pulled into a parking garage below what had looked like the same building where they dropped him off the night before.

He had taken her to his place. Her pulse jumped from the sudden awareness of what he intended to the anticipation of what was to come.

After parking, he opened the door for her and helped her out of the car. His parking spot was steps from the elevator, and she thought he must have some pull to get that coveted spot.

"I should've asked… Are you okay with coming up to my place for the quiet you were seeking?"

He didn't air quote "quiet" with his fingers but it was there in his voice.

Before she could answer, the elevator doors opened and he led her inside.

He pushed the only button for a floor that didn't have a number.

It only had a P on it. He had to slide in an ID card before the elevator would even move. She presumed he lived in the penthouse. But really, she couldn't imagine him in anything less.

He held her hand while the elevator rose. He didn't move her any closer, but for some reason she felt like the prey of a lion being dragged into his lair. Her heart pounded. How could it not? She didn't know him that well… She was taking a risk by going up to his place alone. No one would know she was even there.

The doors whooshed open and, surprisingly, there was no hallway. The elevator opened directly into a wide-open living space. No wonder he had to use an ID card. You wouldn't want just anyone intruding into your personal space.

She looked around and caught her breath. He had half of the top floor to himself. The open area was full of windows, and being that it was dark out, the city's lights were enchanting.

He released her hand and she wandered over to an oversize window. "Wow."

"Yeah, the view was a selling point."

"Can you see the river from here?"

"Yes."

She turned to him, but he was gone. She took in the furnishings and décor. It was simple, but modern and classy. Nothing pretentious. Sleek, clean lines. Beautiful, just like him.

She liked that.

She wandered around the corner and found him in the large open kitchen. She ran her fingers over the granite countertops. The stainless-steel appliances were all high-end chef quality. She loved to cook and would kill for a kitchen like this.

"This is a cook's dream kitchen. Do you cook?" It would be a shame if no one used the kitchen to its utmost potential.

"I dabble. I've taken some cooking classes. I enjoy it, but I wish I was better. You?"

She nodded her head, still in awe of the kitchen. The kitchen was always the heart of a home.

"I love to cook." She added, "And bake. I'm always trying new recipes. I've never taken classes though."

"Maybe you can make me something someday. Wine?"

She would love to cook him a meal. However, like Ren, he was only obligated to tonight's date, so it surprised her that he mentioned the future. But she was elated at the possibility. "Sure."

He gave her a grin. "To the wine or the cooking?"

She laughed. "Both."

He pulled a bottle out of a built-in wine cooler. He uncorked it and poured them each a glass.

He lifted his glass up to her. She tapped hers against his and they both said, "Cheers." Cole added, "...to a fun night." He held out his free hand and said, "Come."

Without hesitation, she linked her hand in his and followed him back through the open great room. He took her glass and his, placing them on a table in front of a large white sectional sofa before sinking his large body into the soft leather cushions. He patted the couch next to him and she followed. It felt how it looked. The leather was quality: luxurious and very comfortable.

"You're not worried about wine stains on your furniture?"

"Should I be? Are you klutzy?" he kidded. He picked up a nearby remote, and with a couple pushes, music came through a hidden surround sound system and the lights dimmed enough to give them a better view of the city.

"Slick," she said.

"Better to seduce you with."

She waved a hand toward the remote. "I guess you're used to groupies throwing themselves at you."

Cole shrugged. "There are women who will do whatever to whomever just for a little fame."

"Ah, that desired fifteen minutes of fame."

"I last way longer than fifteen minutes. I guarantee you."

"Do you think you're so slick that I'm simply going to fall into bed with you?" she teased.

"No, I plan on throwing you on the bed. No falling necessary."

The playful banter turned serious.

"Is that a promise?" Then the heat rose in her cheeks. She'd never been this forward with any man. She had even surprised herself. She jumped to her feet and walked around the couch behind him. Her fists clenched and she couldn't control her sudden tremors.

She didn't want him to see her reaction, to see she was suddenly overcome with nerves. Not that she didn't want to take this further, but she just didn't have the experience to be so open to sex with someone she hardly knew. She never had a one-night stand before, and even though that's not what she intended this evening, it didn't mean that it wouldn't end up being one.

She turned to face the back of him where he still sat on the couch. He hadn't moved an inch. She closed her eyes and steadied her breath. She wanted this. No time to chicken out now. Inhaling a deep, calming breath, she reined in her anxiety.

When she opened her eyes, she saw her reflection in the glass of the wide, long windows.

Damn, he had seen every reaction she's had in the past minute.

But he still hadn't moved. He was waiting on her, no doubt. She had to be the one certain about how this moved forward tonight. She could do this. She *wanted* to do this. And that thought bolstered her confidence.

"Maybe I merely want to be friends." She moved closer behind him, with only the couch separating them. She traced her index finger from one shoulder across his broad back to the other shoulder. "Maybe," she paused, "I just want to rub elbows with the rich and famous."

He suddenly moved as he let out a little snort. "Maybe you should just shut up, get over here, and kiss me."

He grabbed her hand as she moved around the sofa to face him. She stuck a knee between his and pushed them apart. She slid between his parted thighs. Her mischievous smile grew as she leaned in, her face inches from his.

"Maybe..." She placed her palm flat over his heart. "Just maybe..." The steady thumping of his heart quickened. "You should just fuck me."

His eyelids lowered and he released a shuddered breath. "Maybe I just might do that."

Her pussy pulsed at the soft, syrupy sound of his deep voice. She became warmer, wetter. "I want to fuck you on this couch." Her words were slow and breathless.

He laughed. It was low and held promises of naughty things to come.

Eve unbuttoned her blouse, taking her time. Cole ran his hands up her thighs, finding the tops of her stockings and rolling them down her legs one at a time. She kicked off her heels, so he could slide them over her feet, all the while taking the opportunity to caress her ankles, her feet, her toes. She shivered as his hands went back up under her skirt again, finding her silky panties. She peeled her blouse over her shoulders and tossed it on the couch. She watched him through hooded eyes as he slipped her panties over her thighs, her knees, and then over her feet, while pausing to touch her here and there. The panties ended up on top of her stockings. She reached behind her to unhook her bra, letting it fall down her arms. It dropped to the floor and she kicked it out of her way. Their eyes never left each other's. The eye contact was more intimate than she expected, but she couldn't break their gaze. Wearing only her skirt, she climbed over his thighs to straddle him. It pushed up around her waist allowing her bare skin to press against denim.

With a tilt of her hips, her pussy rubbed the length of his hardness under his jeans. Coarse against her tender skin. But, oh, so good. Just enough abrasiveness to make her whimper for his touch there.

With one hand caressing her thigh and the other on her breast, he dipped his head and captured a nipple in his lips.

His mouth was greedy against her skin and she let out a shuddered sigh, and then whimpered when his teeth skimmed her nipple. His fingers worked up her thigh and found her heat. She was wet and ready, and she wanted him to touch her until she came. She wanted, *needed*, a release.

She ground against him, against his fingers, against his denim-clad thighs. She rose and fell as his fingers parted her, smoothing over her clit, exploring her creases. He slid a finger and then two into her, his thumb finding her clit, rubbing it as his fingers fucked her.

Small noises escaped her as his mouth explored her other breast, his tongue flicking at the hard point. Her back bowed, her chest pushed toward him, and her head dropped back, her mouth slack. Her eyes fluttered shut. His mouth was relentless, sucking her nipple as he slid his long fingers in and out of her, taking no prisoners. The building tension deep inside made her cry out. She wanted to beg for mercy, for him to bring her over the edge. As he sank his teeth around her nipple and worked his fingers in and out of her, she tensed as she clamped around his fingers and a wave of an orgasm crashed through and over her. Her hips jumped, but he held her tight against him until she finally collapsed. Boneless. Breathless.

"Fuck," Cole groaned against her ear. He was still as hard as a rock beneath her. With a sudden move, he stood, lifting her off the couch and into his arms. She wrapped her arms around his neck and her bare legs around his waist. She was still weak from the intense orgasm, but he supported her with his arms around her thighs and his hands holding her ass firmly. Like he owned it.

He strode effortlessly under her weight to a door at the far end of the condo. It had been slightly ajar, but he kicked it open with some force. It banged against the doorstop, making her jump just a little.

He threw her onto the bed as promised, making her both squeal and laugh. He turned her over onto her belly. No doubt about it, he was taking charge. He unzipped and pulled off her skirt, not so gently.

This. This is what she wanted. She wanted a man who knew what he wanted and took it with no hesitation.

And there was none as he pulled his shirt over his head and dropped it to the floor. Eve looked back over her shoulder at him because she *so* did not want to miss this.

He took a step back from the bed, which gave her a chance to scramble to the headboard. A thought flickered through her mind that she should be embarrassed she was buck naked with a man she had met only recently. But she pushed the thought away and leaned against the headboard to watch. Now was not the time to second guess her choices. Oh, no. Now was the time to enjoy the bounty in front of her.

Her movement caught his eye and he said, "You're beautiful."

She smiled and said, "So are you."

His chest was broad and muscled nicely. He had a Boston Bulldogs tattoo over the left pectoral muscle, right over his heart. His other shoulder had a huge tribal tattoo, which ran over his shoulder cap, over his right pectoral muscle, and down his arm. The tattoos didn't take away from his muscles or his looks, but enhanced them. And so did being hairless, nothing but a teasing little dark line of hair running from his belly button into his jeans. He clearly took pride in his body and kept working out after retirement. She knew one of his main sources of income was starring in ads and being a spokesperson, so he had no choice but to stay in shape. This was a body he worked at, fought for. She'd seen ads with his six-pack so rock solid that it looked like he had zero body fat. But it didn't look like that here and now. It was there, but not as noticeable, and Eve liked it better that way. He looked like a man, not a superhero with all chiseled muscle. He looked touchable and huggable the way he was right now. Not to mention lickable. *Oh, yes.*

He gave her a quick smile when he reached for the button on his jeans. His fingers hesitated barely above it, teasing her, just like that disappearing line of hair.

"Just do it," she breathed, wanting to see the rest of him so badly.

She was impatient to see all six feet of unadulterated nakedness. Not just what the public saw.

If only the women at the bar could see what she now had in front of her, they would be fighting her tooth and nail.

Where on earth had that come from? She had never been a jealous person like that.

His smile turned broader, and his eyes held a sparkle, pulling Eve away from that thought. She swallowed hard.

"Tell me what you want," he demanded.

Eve released her bottom lip; she hadn't even realized she was biting it. "You. All of you." Everything. Everything he had to offer.

Somewhere between his tossing her on the bed and her sitting against the headboard, he had lost his shoes and socks. She did want to see all of him, but she didn't want to forget the luscious sight she was seeing right now. Cole, shirtless and barefoot, in only a pair of old, worn jeans. She wanted to keep that memory burned in her brain forever. It was the hottest thing she had ever seen.

He unsnapped his jeans and struggled a bit with the zipper as his cock strained against it.

She felt the anticipation like she was a kid unwrapping a Christmas gift and someone had used too much tape.

He bent over to pull his jeans off completely, and when he straightened...

"Damn" escaped her lips. Though the exclamation was more like a whisper, he had heard her.

"Surprised?"

"Uh...no. But I've only seen that size on a..." She trailed off and blushed, horrified where her thoughts went.

"A black man?" he finished for her.

She could only nod. Though the only ones she'd seen had been in movies or photos.

"Been with many black men?"

"No." In fact, she hadn't been with many men in general.

He tilted his head. "Did Ren's size surprise you last night?" He studied her face, waiting to see how she'd answer. She didn't owe him an answer, but gave it to him anyway.

"I didn't see it."

"No?" It was his turn to be surprised. "He must be losing his touch."

Not exactly, she thought. His touch had been more than perfect.

"I'm afraid you think I'm easy." She wouldn't be shocked if he did, especially with her being Ren's date last night and now, here she was getting intimate with Cole tonight.

"Are you?"

Direct and to the point, the question made her squirm inside, but it brought this whole scheme of hers home.

"No."

"How many men have you been with?"

She was stunned he would ask. It was so inappropriate and he clearly had enough manners that he would know it was. She'd only been with less than a handful of men in her life and her anger started to bubble up at his sudden rudeness.

"How many women have you been with?" She turned the tables on him and he simply stared at her, his expression unreadable. "Oh, and how many men?" His lips thinned out and his eyes darkened. "Double digits? Triple? Why is it okay for men to 'sow their wild oats,' but a woman can't? If she enjoys sex, she's considered a whore, or a slut, or *easy*."

He moved around to the side of the bed as he considered her words. "You're right. There's a double standard. There always has been." He reached out for her hand, but she pulled away. "I'm sorry. I shouldn't have pried."

She had expected him to fight back, not concede. Her anger dissipated. "I'm sorry for getting angry."

"You had every right to be."

He reached for her hand again and this time she let him take it.

"If I was a woman, I'd be considered a ho." He laughed, which seemed to lighten the mood between them.

But she wondered about the triple digits. Was it possible? Oh brother! She might have a lot to live up to with his vast experience with *both* sexes. If that didn't shake up her confidence a little.

"I love sex," he confessed as he climbed onto the bed near her feet. "The human body turns me on."

"I do, too. I had someone who taught me to love it. He showed me passion, real passion. I learned that sex is way better when there's intimacy, too."

He grabbed her ankles and slid her down until she was lying on her back. "There's a difference between fucking and making love," Cole said, working his way up her body on his knees. "Sometimes I just need to fuck; I need a release. Other times, I want a long, passionate sex session. I want to take my time and appreciate the person I'm with for who they are, what they enjoy. I want to explore my partner fully. Find out what does it for them. Take them to the brink and back again, until they can't stand it anymore."

She rose to her elbows to get a better view of him straddling her hips. His cock was long and thick and pointing directly at her. "We need to stop talking and appreciate each other," Eve said with a smile and a lick of her lips.

With almost a growl, he grabbed her hips, slid his body between her legs. He propped her legs over his shoulders and he buried his face against her. She gasped as his tongue plunged into her, working in and out. Pleasure danced over her body and landed at her core as his tongue found her clit and licked. He sucked at it while slipping two fingers into her until they couldn't go any further. Eve threw her head back and gripped the bedcover with her fists. His tongue caressed every nook and crease of her pussy as his fingers worked her.

He dipped his finger in her, capturing her wetness. He ran his slick finger over her folds before pressing it against her anus. He circled her, pressing slightly. She had never felt anything like this, had never done anything even close. But he continued to massage her own wetness around her tight hole, pressing harder, then lighter. Never quite breaking the barrier, but massaging her enough to make her cry out and toss her head back.

Her toes curled and pleasure bolted through her as she came, her hips lifting off the bed, tearing her away from his mouth, her clit far too sensitive so soon after the orgasm.

His lips glistened as he smiled up at her from between her thighs. "So responsive. So tasty."

Eve tried to control her breathing to respond, but she gave up and enjoyed the moment of abandonment. Cole crawled over her and dug in the drawer of the bed stand. He tore the condom wrapper with his teeth and quickly sheathed himself.

He turned her over onto her stomach and pulled her hips back. Her pussy throbbed with anticipation. She wanted him deep inside her. She wanted him to fuck her long and hard until she lost her damn mind.

Cole pressed the head of his cock slightly against her slick folds. He slapped her ass, and because she didn't see it coming, she jumped and squealed at the same time as he rammed himself deep within her. He held her hips as still as he was, fully seated within her. Not a move, not a flinch. Eve's body stretched around him, trying to accommodate his size. She lifted herself on her elbows, trying to get a little relief, but he filled her completely.

"God, you're so tight." His voice was strained; his hands trembled on her hips. He released a long, shuddered breath.

She straightened her spine and lifted herself a little higher on her arms.

"Don't...move." His fingers pressed hard into her flesh. "I told you I can last more than fifteen minutes, but I'm not so sure right now."

She looked over her shoulder at him, at the strain on his face. With eyes closed, his jaw was tight, his mouth slightly open. The sight of him so out of control made her clench her muscles, giving him a squeeze. They both cried out, breathing hard.

"Fuck me. Make me come," she pleaded. He was going to drive her nuts if he didn't move soon.

And he did just that. One moment so still, the next he pounded her from behind, sliding in and out of her with abandon, his hips slapping against her ass. She dropped back to her elbows and pressed her forehead against the mattress. He was so hard; she was so wet. She made herself relax and open to him even wider, to accept all of him. When she did that, his rhythm lost a beat and he released a strangled noise.

He reached around and found her clit with his thumb; he circled it and rubbed it until the sensation of an orgasm burst through her like a wave crashing upon rocks. She screamed out as he continued to pound relentlessly, over and over again until she came once more. But this time he came with her, crying out against her back. He struggled to hold her hips up as his cock throbbed deep inside her.

He let her go and she collapsed to the bed, unable to catch her breath. He followed suit beside her, their chests rising and falling at a rapid rate.

A few minutes later, he turned to his side and pulled her against him, laying a kiss on her shoulder.

Once her breathing slowed and her senses returned to her, she looked down the length of his body, appreciating every masculine line and plane of him. His body was the perfect mixture of hardness and softness.

"Did I hurt you?"

She shook her head and he pulled her tighter within his arms.

"I'm sorry I was so rough. You turned me on so much, I got carried away."

She took it as a compliment. "You didn't hear me complaining, did you?"

He chuckled, his body vibrating against her.

He sighed then and pulled away from her. "Sorry, I need to get rid of this." He got up and padded to the master bathroom to dispose of the condom. He returned in seconds and she watched him approach the bed as if he was water and she was dying of thirst.

"No tan lines."

He paused at the edge of the bed. "What?"

"You don't have any tan lines."

He climbed back onto the bed and enveloped her in his arms. "Why would I?"

"Well, your tan is perfect. I'm jealous. I usually just burn. Or freckle."

"It's not a tan. That's just me."

Eve pulled back a little from him and studied his face.

He looked at her directly and said, "I'm light-skinned."

Eve's eyebrows furrowed and she took a second to wrap her brain around what he had said. "Wait. You're black?"

"Technically."

"You don't look black. You look—"

"White—"

"With a really good tan. Your skin tone is beautiful."

"I'm mixed. My father is black, my mother is white, or really from Italian descent. I could pass for white. I do pass for white, but I'm still officially considered black." He air-quoted "officially."

"Officially. Does the *official* label really matter?"

"To some people it does."

"I'm not 'some people.' Your parents made quite a beautiful baby."

He laid a soft kiss against her lips. Eve was shocked when she realized that was their first kiss. They had fucked before they had even kissed!

"You should see my sister. Absolutely gorgeous. Smart as shit too. Her eyes are greener than mine. She could've been a model, but she wanted to go and be a silly astrophysicist." He laughed.

"What? Wow! That's impressive. Your parents must be extremely proud."

"Yeah, but she got all the brains. I became a dumb jock."

Eve couldn't tell if he was joking or not. She hoped he was. He had been a very successful pro football player. "You could model."

"I do sometimes for ads. I get some great gigs, but…"

"But?" She prodded him.

He lifted a shoulder in a half-hearted shrug. "Sometimes I get tired of being in the limelight. It's calmed down some since I retired, but not enough for me."

"So fame isn't all it's cracked up to be?"

His lips pressed into a grim, flat line. "No. But enough about me." He raised her left hand and spun her wedding band around her ring finger. "Now… About this. Should I be nervous some man is going to bust in here and try to kick my ass?"

"No."

"But you still wear his ring." It wasn't a question; it was a statement that felt like a challenge.

"I do."

"Bad breakup?"

"Not exactly."

"Still painful?"

She thought about that for a moment. Yes, her husband's loss was still painful, but it wasn't as fresh anymore. She would always miss him.

"It was very painful for a while. Enough so that I haven't dated since."

"Since…" he prodded.

"His death."

"I'm sorry." Cole wrapped his fingers around hers and pressed her hand against his bare chest, over his Boston Bulldogs tattoo. She felt his heartbeat. It was slow and steady.

"You've apologized way too much tonight."

He gave a slight shrug. "Apologies don't cost a thing."

She turned her head on the pillow to look at him. Really look at him. This man was no dumb jock.

"What?" he asked, like he was suddenly worried she could see his thoughts.

She smiled at him. "Nothing."

"Do you want me to take you home? Or do you want to stay and make me breakfast?" He seemed to emphasize the second question, as if it were his preference.

She wanted to reverse the questions on him. Did he want her to stay or go? But she didn't want to sound like she was unsure of herself…even though she was. What was the normal protocol for this?

"I would love to make you breakfast in that amazing kitchen," she finally said.

"Ah. I see. You only want me for my big kitchen."

She giggled. And then stopped in dismay. She sounded like a giddy schoolgirl!

"You know it." She pulled the pillow out from underneath her head and bopped him in the face with it. "There's nothing like a man and his big kitchen."

He wrestled the pillow away and rolled on top of her, pinning her to the bed. She grabbed the pillow again and started whacking him with it. They laughed so hard they were both out of breath. He finally caught her flailing wrists and pinned them to either side of her face.

"Is that considered a tackle?"

"You don't know much about football, do you?"

"Should I?" She asked.

He made a sound of mock disgust before capturing her lips with his. His lips moved over hers, his tongue pushing between them. Their tongues tangled and the kiss deepened until all the kidding was gone, and nothing remained but naked desire.

He pulled away just enough to say, "There's plenty of time until dawn for me to teach you the fundamentals of football. But first, I want to hear you cry out again when you're coming."

That sounded like a plan she could live with.

CHAPTER 6

Eve moved around the kitchen as if she belonged there. While Cole was in the shower, she cut up the fresh vegetables she found in his crisper bin. He requested a veggie and cheese omelet, with a side of turkey bacon, and lots and lots of coffee. His words, not hers.

The smell of brewing coffee swirled around her as she found the pans and utensils she needed to make him breakfast.

She wore nothing but one of his pale pink button-down collared shirts. It was haphazardly buttoned and the sleeves were rolled up to her elbows since his shirt was way too big for her. She hadn't even bothered to look for her panties. She wasn't sure where they'd ended up.

The morning sunlight lit up the penthouse enough that she hadn't even had to turn on any lights. The skyline was as stunning in the early morning hours as it had been last night.

As she worked in the kitchen, she noticed there were traces of his football career around the condo. Front and center was an enormous photo of Cole and Ren holding the Super Bowl trophy together over their heads, a look of pure joy on their faces. Colorful confetti rained down around them as they both celebrated the biggest win of their lives.

The elevator made a loud *ding* and the doors whooshed open, revealing one of the subjects in the photo. Eve's heart stopped.

Was Cole expecting Ren? Did Ren have the security card for Cole's penthouse?

She felt like a rabbit caught in a snare when Ren looked up and spotted her.

"What the fuck?"

Shit.

A small part of her wanted to run into the bedroom and slam the door shut. But that was just ridiculous. Wasn't it?

Eve was still weighing her options, when Ren walked toward her with a weird look on his face. And by weird she was thinking it was a combination of surprise and anger, mixed with a little disappointment.

"What the fuck!"

Didn't he just say that? Eve simply gave him a crooked smile and tried to swallow the lump in her throat.

"What the hell are you doing here?"

Luckily, before she could answer, Cole came out of the bedroom, wearing loose cotton pants and tying the drawstring at his waist while he walked.

Cole, ignoring the thunderous look on Ren's face, said, "Hey, bro," as if Ren normally walked into his condo at any given time.

And maybe he did. But this morning wasn't the best timing for Eve.

Ren shook his head, closed his gaped mouth, and said, "Tell me you're having a breakfast date."

Eve quickly turned her back on him and busied herself by grabbing the butter, eggs, and milk out of the fridge.

As she turned to place the food on the counter, she practically bumped chests with Ren. He was that close. His tension engulfed her.

He looked her up and down and she could feel the heat in his gaze. She didn't think it was from desire at that moment. He glanced over his broad shoulder at Cole. "Is that your shirt she's wearing?"

Cole shrugged and poured himself a cup of coffee. "Coffee?" he offered.

"You're kidding me, right?"

Ren wasn't talking about coffee either.

He plopped down on one of the bar stools on the other side of the kitchen bar. He threw his car keys on the counter and the loud clatter made Eve start.

"Dude, Eve's making breakfast. Let her make something for you."

Eve finally found her voice, "Yes, let me make breakfast for both of you."

Ren turned his head from Cole to pin her with his gaze.

"You know, Dix, I did not expect this."

"Me neither," Cole answered honestly.

"I actually came over to tell you that I was interested in seeing her again." His gaze never left Eve's face. She schooled herself to keep the surprise off her face.

"You couldn't call?" Cole joked, but it ended up sounding a little flat.

"I'm sorry," Eve told Ren.

Ren shook his head. "No reason to be sorry."

"But if it's any consolation, I would like to see you again, too." She wanted to cringe at her own words. *But if it's any consolation, Ren, I really want to see both you* and *your best friend. Feel better now?*

The sudden silence was so great Eve could hear the butter melting in the fry pan. Both men just stared at her as if she'd grown two heads. She didn't blame them.

"Really," Ren said.

She started cracking eggs into a bowl, avoiding direct eye contact and keeping her hands busy. "Yes. Why not?"

The men looked at each other, then back at her.

Cole cleared his throat. "So, uh, you want another date with Renny?"

"Not only Renny, as you call him, but with you, too. I had a great time last night."

Ren snorted. "It sure looks like you did."

Cole gave him a wide grin. Eve worried that Ren was still a bit too volatile for Cole to be pushing his buttons.

"I did. And I had a great time with you the other night, too. I'd love to see you both." She whipped the eggs and milk together, still not meeting their gaze. "I mean, if you both don't mind."

Once again the silence was deafening. She was afraid to look.

If they rejected the idea of her dating them both, her plan would never work. It was better to know now, wasn't it?

Cole set a cup of steaming coffee next to her. "Creamer?"

She nodded her head and he poured some into her mug and stirred it for her. She peeked up at him. His face was as blank as he could keep it.

"Sugar?"

Ren let out a frustrated sound. "Cole, damn it, you're such a dick."

He looked at Ren in surprise. "Why? Because the thought of her seeing both of us doesn't bother me?"

"Yes! No!" He groaned. "Fuck! I don't know."

"Who cares? Just wear a fucking condom."

"Just wear a fucking condom," Ren repeated. He shook his head. "Just that simple then?"

"Yeah, why the fuck not?"

"We have never dated, or even slept with, the same woman."

Cole gave him a direct look. "So?"

"Cole, grab some plates, please?"

He did what Eve asked, setting them next to the stove. She turned to Ren. "Bacon?"

"Is it that shitty turkey bacon he buys?"

Eve laughed, breaking the tension in the room. "Yes."

"What man eats turkey bacon?"

"Me," Cole answered and shoved a piece into this mouth right from the pan.

"You're such a pussy," Ren said.

"Eve, was I a pussy last night?"

Eve gave him a sideways look. "I made scrambled eggs with veggies and cheese instead of omelets since there are three of us."

"It better not be that tofu cheese," Ren told him.

"No, I threw that shit out. That was nasty."

Both men finally laughed and Eve relaxed a bit.

As they all ate their breakfast, the question of her seeing both men never quite got answered. They skirted the issue and talked about everything but. Eve could see the comradery between the two of them. She didn't want to do anything to screw that up.

CHAPTER 7

After breakfast was finished and the pot of coffee almost empty, the guys cleaned up, since she'd cooked. It was only right, they said. And she wasn't going to question it.

Then, surprisingly, Ren offered her a ride home. She wasn't sure if he just wanted to get her out of Cole's penthouse, but he offered. She accepted. And Cole hadn't argued.

The ride home had been a bit stilted. But he acted like a complete gentleman the whole way.

Eve was afraid that Ren knowing she had sex with his best friend would put him off. Would he sever the ties before she could even propose her daring plan? It would only be a normal reaction, right?

After he pulled into her driveway in front of her little house in the suburbs, he shut the Escalade off and turned to her.

Before he could even say anything she spoke. "I can make it up to you."

His brows rose. "How?"

"Do you have to ask?"

"So you were serious about seeing both of us?"

"I would like that."

He shook his head as he said, "I'm not sure I can go along with that. But I'm willing to get together again to see what we have." He snagged a tendril of her hair and twisted it around his finger. "I like you."

"I like you, too." She gave him a half smile. "How about next Friday night?"

He was silent as he studied her face.

"Only if you give me the chance to show you my place, since you've seen Cole's."

She met his gaze. "It's not a competition." She needed them to work as a team, not compete against each other.

Ren snorted. "You're dealing with two very competitive men. Of course, it's a competition. Something as simple as buying a round of drinks turns into a competition."

"A lot of testosterone to burn, huh?"

"That too." He brushed his thumb over her bottom lip. "I knew you would have freckles over your nose."

All her makeup had worn off from the previous night's activities. And, of course, not expecting an overnight stay with Cole, she had nothing with her to fix it.

"Where else do you have freckles?"

She gave him a slow smile. "You're going to have to find out for yourself."

"Oh, that sounds like a challenge I will enjoy."

He climbed out of the SUV and went around to open her door. "You're on for Friday. I'll text you my address and the time."

She walked to her door before he called out, "Wear something really sexy."

She smiled and waved as she unlocked the door and escaped from his heated gaze.

And now, here she was—less than a week later—staring out of a car window, watching the scenery fly by, after giving the Uber driver Ren's address. The driver took her out to the suburbs northwest of the city. He drove her through a neighborhood of tree-lined roads, well-manicured lawns, and enormous homes.

The driver slowed, reading the house numbers, but they weren't on the mailboxes. No. The ornate numbers appeared on each *gated* driveway. Finally, he pulled up to a gate and pushed the button embedded in a stone pedestal.

The gate opened automatically and the driver proceeded up the lane to a large circle in front of the house. Eve pressed her forehead to the glass to look up, to see how immense the house was. Of course, it was ridiculously big.

She jerked away from the glass when the front door opened and Ren jogged down the gray stone steps to grab her door. He helped her out, but she turned back to the car.

"Hold on," she told him. "I have to pay the driver."

"Stop." He waved a hand toward her and pulled out his wallet. He paid the driver who then mentioned he was a big fan and asked for an autograph. Ren's smile widened and he obliged. He shook the driver's hand before he drove out of the gate, beeping and waving. Ren clearly appreciated his fans.

Ren chuckled and then turned his attention to Eve. "You don't have a car?"

"No. No reason to. It's cheaper for me to take taxis and car services."

Ren whistled long and low. "Wow. No way, I like my freedom of just jumping in a vehicle and going at any moment."

Eve shrugged. "It works for me."

Ren stepped back and got an eyeful of Eve. "And that dress works for me. Hot damn."

She had decided to wear her emerald-green two-piece dress with the plunging neckline and a bottom hem that barely covered her ass. Like the dress she wore to the commitment ceremony, her shoulders were completely bare. The only thing holding the top up was two thin spaghetti straps. And the bottom? The swell of her hips. Occasionally a sliver of her midriff would show when she moved. The dress was simple, but effective. And paired with the emerald-green strappy heels she wore, she could see how effective it was on Ren.

He leaned in to kiss her shoulder. "I had to kiss that freckle." He held his hand out to her and she linked her hand with his. "I plan on tasting every freckle on your body, just so you know."

"I look forward to it."

He led her up the steps and into the house. House. No, it wasn't just a house. It was a house on steroids.

The foyer, more like a grand entrance, was two stories high with a chandelier in the shape of an octopus. It looked as though it was made of a dark metal, brass maybe, with a light fixture hanging off each tentacle. How odd.

"That's different."

"I love steampunk."

Steampunk. So not how she thought of him. She expected his home to have clean lines, modern décor, almost similar to Cole's penthouse. But after he mentioned steampunk she could spot it in the actual architectural design of the house. From the staircase in the foyer that led up to the second floor down to the smallest furnishings. Lots of metals and woods, from dark browns to light golds. Gears and pulleys. Steamer trunks. A mix of gothic, industrial, and Victorian style. Definitely not what she was expecting.

He took her through a large room, which could have been a living room or sitting room. Either way, it could have housed a small family. Dark leather sofas flanked a large stone fireplace.

This house was dark compared to Cole's light penthouse. Such complete opposites.

He led her to the other end of the large room to French doors. He opened them both wide and escorted her through to an enormous deck. She wandered away from him over to the rail of the deck, which overlooked a private lake. She absorbed the beauty of the water and the scenery. It felt…peaceful. Trees and wood fence lined both sides of his well-cared-for lawn, giving a sense of privacy from any neighbors. She could see herself spending a lot of time outdoors, if this were her property.

"I thought we could have dinner out here. The deck faces west. We'll be able to see the sunset."

She turned and he was standing next to a table that had lit candles and plates covered with cloches. Cloches? Steampunk? Who was this man?

She said, surprised, "Did you cook?"

Ren laughed. "Be thankful I didn't. I have a friend who is an awesome chef. She made us a special meal."

"Are you trying to seduce me, Mr. Landis?"

He laughed again. "Not at all, Ms. Sanders. But…" He pulled her closer and gazed down at her. "Is it working?"

"The night is young, Mr. Landis. We shall see. We shall see."

He waved a hand toward the table. "Let's eat before it gets too cold." He pulled a chair away from the table. "Please sit."

She did, and he pushed the chair closer to the table for her.

"Krug Brut?" Ren asked. "It's a 1988, a very good year."

"What?"

He chuckled, and pulled a bottle of champagne from a silver bucket full of ice. He showed her the label before he popped the cork and poured.

She lifted her glass, clinking it with his. "Cheers! Do you even remember 1988?"

"Barely."

She took a sip and the bubbles made her scrunch her nose. "Mmm. That is so good."

"Your face says otherwise."

"No, it's really good, the bubbles tickled my nose."

"I kept that bottle for a special occasion."

She looked at him in shock. "Really?"

So, it was probably an expensive bottle of bubbly... Did he really feel like tonight was an occasion worth opening a vintage bottle of champagne? He kept surprising her, keeping her on her toes. He was so not a typical jock.

"What are you smiling at?" he asked her.

"Nothing."

"No, that wasn't nothing."

She gazed toward the lake, avoiding his eyes. "I was merely surprised that you'd think a dinner with me would be a special occasion."

He covered her hand with his, where she had it laying on the table. "Don't discount yourself."

"Are you sure you were a football player?"

"I'm trying to show you my gentler side, the manners my momma taught me. Later, I'll show you my beast side. The animalistic side where I'm going to tear off your dress and fuck you like you've never been fucked before." He growled like a tiger, which made her giggle.

"You sure we need to eat dinner first?"

He laughed. "Yes, Adelia would kill me if the gourmet dinner she prepared went to waste. And I do want to watch the sunset with you first. It's beautiful, I promise." He pulled the cloche off her plate and said, "'All must eat to live and nourish one another.'"

"What's that from?"

He shrugged and unveiled his own meal. "I heard it somewhere and I liked it. It stuck." He indicated the food. "Grilled lamb chops, grilled asparagus, and polenta. Grilled, of course."

She took a bite of the lamb. It was succulent.

"By the look on your face, I think it's safe to say you like lamb."

"I hardly eat it, but this is perfect. Wow. Thank the chef."

"I actually wanted her to make my favorite dish, but she thought this would pair better with the champagne."

"What's your favorite dish?"

"She makes an awesome gourmet burger, with a side of hand-cut fries doused in malt vinegar. Mmm. Mmm. Mmm. And then she makes the best homemade coleslaw ever. Her food is orgasm quality."

"Wow. That does sound good!"

"Next time."

Yes, next time. If there was a next time. Eve sure hoped to hell there was a next time. The man sitting across from her kept her guessing. He was like an onion with so many layers. She wanted to be able to peel all those layers away, to discover all his nuances. If he'd let her.

With full bellies, they moved over to a cushioned love seat on the deck that faced the water. The croak of the bullfrogs and chirp of the crickets serenaded them as they waited for the sun to lower. The colors in the sky reminded her of a painting. It was peaceful and serene.

The man next to her was solid, his arm wrapped around her bare shoulders. She leaned into him, practically tucked under his arm. She pressed her face into his neck and inhaled him, his scent. He smelled so good. She detected a fresh smell of what she thought might be honey...and oatmeal?

"Why do you smell like breakfast?" she murmured against his skin. His deep chuckle sent a shiver up her spine, hardening her nipples.

"It's my soap. It's locally made with honey, oatmeal, and goat's milk. Are you cold?"

"No. Is it also made up with the tears of angels? Because you smell like heaven to me."

Ren snorted. "Oh, you got jokes." He squeezed her and lowered his face, kissing her hard, taking complete possession of her mouth and tongue.

Eve's wrapped a hand around the back of his head, and moaned into his mouth. Their tongues danced together, their breaths mingled. She closed her eyes to sink deeper into the kiss.

Her other hand found his waist, trying to get even closer, if it was possible. His hands slid over her bare back, over her shoulders and down both arms until he got to her wrists. He pulled himself free and pulled back away from her slightly.

"Baby, unless you want me to take you right here, right on this deck, we need to hold off a bit. I promised you a beautiful sunset. Once the sun is down, all bets are off."

Eve didn't know if she could wait that long. Her breathing was strained and she was already wet. "How soon is the sun going down?"

Ren let out a ragged breath. "Damn, you're not making this easy for me. We need to stand up." He grabbed her hand to help her up. "I'm hard as fuck." He adjusted himself in his tailored black slacks. He guided her to the deck rail. She leaned her belly against it, and he stood behind her, his hips tight against her ass. "Can you feel me?"

Eve's breath caught; she could only nod.

Ren swept her hair to one side and nuzzled her neck. He worked his way down, kissing and licking her heated skin, then nipping her where her neck met her shoulder. He wrapped his arms around her waist, the weight of her breasts against his forearms. He leaned his cheek against hers.

"There. See that? Mother Earth is going to bed for the night. She's giving us all those amazing colors as a goodnight."

"It's beautiful."

"It never gets old."

They watched as the sun lowered until it slowly disappeared behind the horizon, the vibrant colors slowly turning to hues of dark blue, gray, and black.

Her heart skipped a beat when he grabbed her hand and escorted her back through the house. He led her to the impressive staircase in the foyer.

"That's a lot of stairs," she teased.

"Do you want me to carry you?"

"I thought you'd never ask!"

When he swung her up into his arms, she squeaked in surprise. She could feel the rumble of his laughter in his chest.

She lightly punched him in the arm. "I was only kidding!"

His biceps flexed, and she smoothed a hand over the muscle as he climbed the stairs with ease, even under her weight.

"So strong," she said, laughing. "So manly!"

He gave her a look, trying to appear serious and "manly," but failing.

He strode down the hall, carefully carrying her through the door of what she assumed was his bedroom. *Bedroom* wasn't quite the right description. It was more like a suite. Okay, not even that. More like a small apartment, since the average bedroom doesn't have a sitting area near a stone fireplace. She got a glimpse of a walk-in closet the size of her own modest bedroom. And the en suite bathroom? She couldn't wait to see it. She bet it had a shower big enough for a Slip 'N Slide. But it would have to wait.

As he approached the bed, she expected him to dump her on it. But he didn't. He gently lowered her to her feet on the hardwood floor.

She turned in awe of his headboard. "Wow, you really take this steampunk seriously."

"You like it?"

The headboard was massive, but a showpiece. It was clutches, gears, pistons, and exhaust manifolds, all pieced together and welded into an interesting piece of art. All in powder coating, giving it a dull black appearance. Very masculine, like him.

"It's crazy. And I mean crazy good. My dad was a big car buff. He would've loved this."

"Believe it or not, a fan made this for me. He found the scrap parts in a junkyard, welded it all together, and there you go."

"How did he know you liked steampunk?"

"A piece was written about me in one of the sports magazines.

The writer came here for the interview and took some pictures of my house. Not even six months later, this was delivered to my door. The note said it was a thank-you for bringing the Super Bowl trophy home to Boston for the first time ever."

"Did he at least get an autograph?"

"Oh yeah. I sent him a nice package of autographed items."

She wandered over to one of the floor-to-ceiling windows. She could see the moon just rising enough to reflect off the water.

Ren stepped up behind her, running his fingers down her arm, from shoulder to fingertips, and back up again. He grasped her shoulders and turned her around, so she had to look up into his face.

He reached out and brushed her hair over her shoulder. His mouth opened, as if he were having a hard time forming a sentence. "I'm trying so hard not to be a beast right now."

A beast.

A shiver ran up Eve's spine, puckering her nipples even harder. Enough to be painful.

She fought the urge to rub them, to soothe them. To circle her fingers around her own nipples, inviting him to take over.

Ren stared at her intensely as she searched his features, his face.

"You're a very handsome man, you know. I'm going to touch you."

"Only if you're prepared for the consequences," he warned her.

"Would I touch you if I wasn't?"

She traced her fingers over his brow. His eyes were large and a deep, dark brown. His nose was broad and a little crooked, probably from playing football all those years. At the corner of his left eye was a little scar. A result from rough game play? His ears were perfectly shaped; the square cut diamond studs in his ear were enormous, like his house. They must be two carats each, by her estimate. They seemed to be the only jewelry he was wearing. Or what she could see, since he was currently still overdressed for her taste.

She ran a thumb over his bottom lip and he caught it between his teeth. His smile was so bright in contrast to his rich, dark chocolate skin tone. His cheek bones and his chin were chiseled and strong. His face was broad and one hundred percent male. From his chin, she moved her hands along each side of his jawline. It was powerful and distinct, like she imagined the rest of his body was. She cupped her right hand around the front of his throat, his Adam's apple jumping beneath her palm. Her left thumb stroked across his perfectly shaped lips again.

His eyelids had lowered during her exploration, barely hiding the heat behind them. When she was done and he finally looked at her, the heat had turned into raw passion. A slight tic pulsed in his jaw.

She tilted her head as she studied him, and without thought, she murmured, "There is a saying: the blacker the berry the sweeter the juice."

She barely heard his response. His moist breath washed over her thumb. She finally started to pull her hand away, but he caught her wrist.

"I'm sorry. I didn't realize I said that out loud. That was extremely inappropriate." Her apology was a breathless whisper, the words catching slightly. But she didn't care if what she said was inappropriate, because under her right palm, which was still tightly pressed against his throat, his pulse was beating even faster.

"Tupac's lyrics in one of his songs. 'Keep Ya Head Up.'"

The harder he held her left wrist to keep her thumb against his lips, the tighter her right hand wrapped around his neck.

Heavily muscled and sinewy, this was not a throat that could be easily crushed. Hot blood pulsed strongly through pronounced veins.

Ren Landis was built like a bull.

She had no doubt his hand could crush her wrist with no effort at all.

He was strong and solid.

And she wanted to see him naked.

He wanted to see her naked, spread open over his bed. Soft thighs, curvy hips, handfuls of breasts. *Damn*. She had it going on.

Her hand on his throat was tight, and restricting his breathing a little, but he liked it. He had a raging hard-on like no other.

"You like to play rough?" he asked her.

She gave a little shrug and the tips of her fingers dug into his skin a little deeper. "I don't know." A little nervous laugh escaped her. She was so playing with fire!

He reached down, grabbed her ass, and lifted her up and against him, making sure she felt his hard length. "You don't know?" He spun her around, breaking her grip. He placed her on the bed on her knees, facing her away from him.

She shook her head, her hair sweeping down her back. It was long and silky and he wanted to grab fistfuls of it and bend her to his will.

He bent close to her ear and growled, "We'll see how rough you like it."

She made a little noise, and, since she hadn't said no, he slipped the top of her smoking hot dress over her head, revealing what he already knew. She wore no bra. She had full, luscious breasts but they were still perky enough that she could go without support. And he liked that she was bold enough to go without. Nothing wrong with a woman with natural breasts. Just how he liked them.

He reached around to cup both breasts, squeezing them slightly, his thumbs rubbing over her hard nipples.

"I'm going to pinch them, twist them, and later I'm going to bite them. Do you want that?"

Again, he only heard a small noise, which sounded like encouragement to him. He kissed along her shoulders as he played with her nipples, doing what he said he would. He pinched the hard tips before rolling them between his thumbs and fingers. He twisted them a little harder, pushing her until she cried out, not in pain, but a low sound of pleasure.

She wanted more. And that made his balls tighten and his cock twitch within his pants.

"Turn around."

She did as she was told and she turned to face him on her knees at the edge of the bed. Her face was flushed and her eyes were glazed. And she wore a bit of a distracted smile.

"Get on your back."

She pulled her legs from out beneath her, putting them on each side of his where he stood. She lay back.

"Hips up."

Ren reached underneath her to find the zipper at her waist and slide it slowly down, releasing the snug fabric. He wiggled the dress over her hips and down her thighs. No thigh-high stockings tonight. It was somewhat of a pity since those stockings were hot, but the skin on her legs was flawless and smooth, and, yes, he could find some freckles. His hands slid along her skin as he slid the bottom of the outfit down to her ankles and over her heels.

Now she was only in panties and her heels. Almost completely naked on his bed. His heart felt like it would pound out of his chest. He inhaled deeply and slowly in an attempt to slow himself down.

He debated whether to strip her totally naked or to leave the shoes and panties on for a little longer.

His fingers fumbled with each button on his dress shirt in his rush to get it off and he finally threw it to the side. He unbuckled his leather belt, and with a quick pull, he yanked it from the belt loops and threw it in the same direction as his shirt.

He kicked off his shoes and socks at the same time as he unbuttoned and unzipped his slacks, sliding them down and discarding them.

As anxious as he was to get undressed, he paused when he noticed Eve was watching him. He looked down and saw how hard he was through his tight boxer briefs.

"Take these off me."

She obliged, hooking her fingers into the waistband and slowly, ever so slowly, sliding them down his wide thighs. Her eyes never left his cock.

He kicked them off and said, "Suck me."

He still stood between her legs and she shifted closer to him. Eve's fingers wrapped at the root of his cock.

And squeezed. *Sweet mother!*

A pearly drop of precum escaped.

She bowed her head and licked it up.

Fuuuuuck.

Her lips captured the end and she licked around the edge, before slowly taking him deeply into her warm, wet mouth. The sensation was unbelievably fucking hot.

She made a noise when she got to her limit, when she couldn't take any more of him in. But she held him there for a second, two, three, before pulling her head up just enough to take a breath and then deep throated him again.

Holy fuck. He was going to lose it!

He fought the urge to thrust deeply, all-out fuck her mouth. But he wanted to. Oh, did he want to. He dug his fingers into her hair, grabbing two handfuls. The little sounds she made as she sucked him almost threw him over the edge.

She squeezed her fist harder around the base of him, causing his cock to become a deeper purple. Her mouth was a wet vessel for his length, her tongue lapping the tip on each lift of her head.

"Stop!" Ren cringed internally; that had come out much louder than what he had intended. But if she didn't stop, she would get a throat full of his cum. He wasn't made of steel.

The first time he came with her, he wanted to be deep inside her.

He backed away from her and went to the top of the bed, tucking a pillow behind him as he leaned against the metal headboard and settled himself.

"Panties off, shoes off. Then come to me." His cock was so hard. He was going to have to keep his cool so he wouldn't blow his load in thirty seconds.

Ren watched Eve stand up in her heels, her legs appearing longer than they actually were; she slowly slid her panties off.

Her body was so damn luscious. She only left a little strip of hair above her pussy and he wanted to bury his face there. But he could only take so much at this point. Again, it would have to wait for next time. He looked forward to pleasuring her, and could imagine her rolling around, gasping, and moaning as he ravished her pussy with his mouth.

He closed his eyes, trying to get that picture out of his head. It wasn't helping.

When he opened them, she was shoeless by the side of the bed, climbing onto the mattress.

He held his hand out to help her balance, and she climbed up and over him, straddling his lap.

"Your body is gorgeous," she told him. He worked hard to stay in shape, and he appreciated the compliment.

"Yours, also. I was just thinking how next time I want to eat you out until you come in my mouth."

She wiggled slightly in his lap, probably getting the same image as he was.

Her pussy was hot and damp against his skin, and with a slight shift he could have his cock at her opening.

She leaned close and they met halfway, kissing. They sucked each other's tongues and lips, and nibbled at each other's mouths. Her breasts pressed against his chest, the tight tips pushing against his skin.

She rose just enough to place her wet crease along his length. Then ground down against him as he kissed her.

He grabbed her hips, holding her still. He pulled away enough to say, "Hold on."

His long arms made him able to just reach the drawer of his bed stand and he pulled a string of condoms out. They didn't call him "Long-Arm" Landis for nothing!

Her eyes widened. "Will we need that many?"

He let out a low rumble. "I hope so."

Oh, he fucking hoped so.

He ripped one open, reaching underneath her to encase his oh-so-ready cock.

Please don't let me embarrass myself by losing it within a few seconds!

His balls were so tight, and his cock so hard, that when she guided him into her, he cried out in relief. She settled deeply and he could feel her walls pulsating around him. Her muscles rippling up and down his length.

It felt so fucking good and she hadn't even moved yet!

She wrapped her arms around his neck and she placed her mouth against his ear and said, "I'm going to fuck you so good."

"Fucking ride me" was the only thought he could spit out.

And she did.

With a lift of her hips, she moved up and down his length, the warmth and tightness of her pussy making him close his eyes and blow out a breath.

His hands gripped her sweet, round ass as she continued to move. Then she shifted her hips and he hit *that* spot. His hips moved in rhythm with hers, making sure he stimulated her G-spot over and over. Her juices spilled over him, soaking him, running down his thighs. She was amazing. He had never had a woman who could get this wet, give him everything she had. As she dropped her head back and arched her back, she screamed, "I'm coming!"

He bit the top of her breast and then sucked her nipple into his mouth. The pulsations around his cock made him even harder. He tried to drown out her cries, to concentrate on keeping himself together. He didn't want to lose it. He wanted this pleasure to continue. And continue.

Her body relaxed after her orgasm, and she dropped her forehead against his. "Wow."

"Want another one?"

"Yes."

He quickly flipped her onto her back, her head at the end of the bed. He grabbed a pillow and shoved it under her hips. He settled between her legs. "You want me to fuck you some more?"

"Yes, please."

He held the head of his cock right at her opening, brushing it along her swollen folds. "Do you want me to fuck you hard?"

"Please."

"That's my intent: to please you."

She reached out for him, running her hands over his chest. Her fingers played with his nipples, making him shiver.

"I want to fuck you hard. I want to eat you out. I want to fuck that sweet ass of yours. But right now, I'm going to make you come again. And again and again until you cry for mercy."

He took his time pushing his way into her until he was fully seated. She took all of him. Every inch. She fit him like a glove, like her pussy had been made for him. Only him.

He did a little wiggle with his hips and she cried out.

With the pillow under her hips, she was at the perfect angle for him to hit all the spots he needed to hit with each stroke: her clit and her G-spot. They were his tonight.

He slowly pulled all the way out of her and she made a noise that sounded like a complaint. Again, he slowly seated himself deeply, then once again withdrew completely. The slow strokes frustrated her. She dug her nails into his ass, trying to encourage him to fuck her faster, harder, deeper.

He didn't think she could get any wetter, but she did. When he could no longer take the long, slow strokes either, he pulled out once more.

He dipped his head and drew a nipple into his mouth. He carefully caught the tip between his teeth with enough pressure to bring her to that edge of painful pleasure.

"Fuck me… Fuck me hard," she groaned.

With a push of his hips, he drove himself hard, deep inside her. Hitting the limit of her walls. Again and again until her body clamped down on his cock. And once again, he could feel the waves of another orgasm riding along his length. He fought hard not to come with her. Once she caught her breath, he fucked her relentlessly. Giving no mercy and she asked for none. She came again and again like he promised until he finally had to give up the good fight. When he felt her body tense one more time, he let himself go. He cried out along with her.

And then they were still, their bodies slick with sweat, their pulses pounding, their breathing rapid.

But it was all good. He dropped his head on her shoulder and tried to steady his breath.

"Sorry, I'll move as soon as I can."

She wrapped her arms around his waist. "You're fine."

"Not really, 'cause I need to collapse and I'll crush you." He tried to laugh but it only came out sounding hoarse and breathless. And plus, he didn't want her to see his arms shaking.

With a grunt, he fell beside her on the bed. He gathered her into his arms, pinning her to his side. He laid a kiss on her forehead.

Her hand stroked his hairless chest. He kept it hairless to show the results of his hard workouts. Her finger traced over the Boston Bulldogs tattoo on his right bicep. He waited for her to say something about Cole having the same tattoo. But, she didn't. She was smart enough not to mention the other man she'd recently slept with—who happened to be his best friend—while she was still naked in his bed.

With a groan, he released her to go get rid of the condom. In the bathroom, he looked at himself in the mirror. What was he going to do now? The sex had been amazing. Would she want to see him again? He sure wanted to see her again. Fuck her again. Maybe plan a real date, take her to a fancy restaurant, or a drive along the shore, or…whatever. Something. Anything. He wanted to spend more time with her, get to know her better. But did Cole want the same thing? Were they really in competition for her? That was absolutely crazy. He'd never needed to compete with anyone for a woman, especially his best friend. If a woman didn't want him, no big deal. They could leave, he wouldn't stop them. There were too many women out there to fight over one.

He wouldn't do it. He wouldn't. He put both of his hands against the mirror and took one last good look at himself before dropping his head and letting out a long breath.

Fuck.

CHAPTER 8

For the next few weeks, she continued to see both Ren and Cole. They went on real dates, as well as to functions. But it was always separately. She was enjoying the time she spent with each of them. Even though they were best friends and former teammates, they were still different from each other. Cole was light and fun, and didn't take life so seriously. Ren was also just as fun, but tended to be darker and, at times, he could get very serious. And he definitely liked to be in charge, much more of an alpha personality than Cole. She loved both the differences and the similarities between the two.

But the overwhelming enormity of what she was trying to accomplish with her two guys—and she was starting to consider them as *hers*—scared her. She considered giving up on her plan, but she had gone too far now to want to abandon it. However, what was at stake if she failed ate at her.

She could destroy their friendship, for one. And that would kill her. She didn't want to be responsible for that.

Two, she could alienate them both. And she so did not want to do that. If she did, neither might want to see her again. Ever.

But there were no rewards without risk, right? That was

something her husband had always told her as he would leave for another stint in the jungle to bring medical care to the needy.

The sex was great with the two of them. No, not just great, it was mind-blowing. But seeing them separately was not what she had intended. She wanted both men. At the same time. She wanted to make it a threesome. Not just an awkward love triangle.

She needed to figure out a way to make that happen.

And as she tapped her finger on her cheek, she suddenly figured out what she needed to do next...

She found her cell and texted them both, but separately, so neither could see she had texted the other.

I'm heading out to a friend's beach house for a long weekend. You care to join me? I'll make it worth your while. Just text me a yes and I'll text you back the details.

As she pressed send, a thrill ran through her. She didn't know if it was from nervousness, or excitement, or a bit of both.

She hoped this worked...

E ve paced and checked the time on her cell phone. *Again.* She checked to see if she had missed any calls or texts. She cursed herself. Of course, she hadn't. The phone hadn't left her hand since she had arrived at the house on the beach.

The weather was perfect, a nice breeze coming off the water. Not cold enough for a sweater, but not hot enough to turn on the ceiling fans.

She opened most of the windows to air the place out. It had been a while since anyone had been there and it had felt a little stuffy when she first arrived. There was a line of glass doors along the side of the house facing the water. She slid most of those open, bringing the outside in.

She needed to let out some of the nervous energy coiled inside her. She went out to the deck and leaned against the rail to watch the waves beat along the shore. Her stomach felt like it was taking a beating, too.

Her hand was gripped so tightly around her cell phone that she forced her cramped fingers to relax, and in doing so, she watched in horror as it dropped one story down into the sand.

"Damn it!"

"That's not quite the reaction I expected when I arrived. I was invited, remember?"

Ren laughed and took her in his arms to hold her close and give her a kiss hello. His lips were warm and inviting. She sank into his kiss and his arms, but it had little calming effect on her. She smoothed her hands down his broad back, and he squeezed her ass in her shorts before releasing her. Almost reluctantly.

"I dropped my phone in the sand."

"I can get it for you." He stepped over to the deck rail to peer over. "Damn. That was quite a drop. But I see it."

He gave her another squeeze and a quick kiss on her shoulder before she pointed the way to the steps leading down to the beach.

As he walked away, she watched not only his tight ass, but the thick muscles in his thighs strain the fabric of his Bermuda shorts. Slip-on shoes and a light, loose button-down shirt finished off his look, and it looked perfect on him. She watched him disappear down the steps and let out a long, loud breath.

A movement in the corner of her eye caught her attention. She turned to see Cole, coming through the house toward her. Maybe she shouldn't have left the front door unlocked. She wasn't quite ready for him. She hadn't been sure who would show up first, but she had hoped to say something to the first arrival, so the other man's appearance wasn't a complete surprise.

Too late now.

She hurried into the house while Ren was still retrieving her cell phone.

"Wow, this place is great! What a view! And right on the beach. Your friend must be rolling in the dough to have this place."

"Yeah, I love it here." She grabbed his arm as he moved toward the deck to try to steer him away. "But Cole, hold on a minute. I need to tell you something…"

"What's the matter, babe? This is going to be a great weekend. I've been looking forward to it all week. The beach and this place to ourselves. You to myself. Can't ask for anything more."

"What the fuck?"

Eve tensed at the tone. *Oh, here we go.*

Cole and Eve turned at the same time to see Ren striding with purpose toward them, a dark look on his face.

"What the fuck are you doing here?" He asked Cole. He turned to Eve before Cole could answer. "What the fuck is he doing here?"

Cole held his hands out in front of him, like he was ready to hold Ren back if he came after him. "Dude, I was invited."

Ren slowly turned his head and pinned Eve with his gaze. He said, soft and slowly, "I was invited, too."

Eve squirmed under his gaze, the heat rushing to her face. She hadn't quite pictured this happening. She cursed herself for not planning the meeting better. They knew she was seeing them both, but really, was there any good way to approach what she was going to propose? It was best just to rip off the Band-Aid. It'll sting for a little bit, but then…

She walked toward the empty fireplace, crossing her arms over her chest. When she got to the fireplace—a safe distance away—she turned to face them.

"Sorry. Yes, I invited you both." They both started to say something, but Eve raised her shaky hands to stop them. "Please… Please let me finish."

Neither had moved and they merely stared at her. Cole's expression was blank, while Ren looked a little peeved. Well, possibly more than a little.

"Maybe you both should sit down?"

Cole moved around to take a seat on the couch. Of course, he'd be the amiable one. Ren stood there, shaking his head, his fists

closed. She expected him to be more difficult, since he was more…
heterosexual. Alpha. Stubborn.

She perched on the end of a cushioned chair, like a bird ready to
fly away at the first sign of a predator. "I like men." Well, that was a
lame start. She shook herself mentally and began again. "I've loved
spending time with both of you. Both of you each have something
different to offer. And I really appreciate that about you two."

Ren looked like he was about to say something, so she hurried
on. *Just rip off the damn Band-Aid! You're making a complete mess of this.*
"I love monogamy. When it came to my marriage I loved belonging
to my husband and him belonging to me." She lifted a hand to stop
Ren again. "However…" She grimaced. Once again she sounded like
a bumbling fool. "I don't know how to explain it. You can love
someone deeply, but still want…more?"

Oh, boy. Foot meet mouth. Maybe she should've written a speech
on notecards.

She didn't want them to think that either of them were
inadequate in any way. That was not her intent at all.

Was she being selfish, wanting them both and expecting them to
accept it? Maybe. But they could always say no.

Cole sat up a little straighter. He said, "So you want to continue
to date both of us." At the same time Ren said, "You're dumping
me…us."

Ren finally came around the couch to sit beside Cole. He rubbed
a hand over his short hair, then crossed his arms over his chest, his
expression closed.

"Yes," she answered Cole. Well, sort of. *Oh, boy.* To Ren she said,
"No, not at all."

The guys looked at each other, a flash of confusion crossing both
of their faces.

Ren sighed. "But you're already doing that. I'm not thrilled about
it, but I figured you'd sort it out in the end. I guess…" He frowned.

"So are you looking for some type of schedule?" Cole asked her.

"No, not exactly."

Ren shook his head, the light reflecting off one of his earrings. His brow furrowed. "Spit it out."

"Look at it like a puzzle. Out of the box, we're just random pieces, but together... together those pieces make it complete. Each piece unique, but still they fit. They still need each other to complete the picture." Heat crept up her cheeks. She placed her palms against them, but they were no relief. They were just as hot, if not more so. And worse, damp. "I want both of you."

"We got that part."

"*Both* of you..." she emphasized, lifting her eyebrows. She reminded herself why she could never be a doctor like her late husband. She couldn't even rip off a Band-Aid neatly.

Ren's nostrils flared as he finished her thought in a rough whisper, "At the same time."

Silence.

Her heartbeat pounded at her temples. *Thump, thump, thump.*

The silence around her grew as she stared between them carefully, not quite meeting either of their eyes. "What they have."

"They." It was a statement, not a question that spilled from Ren's lips.

"They?" Cole asked, confused.

Ren sat back and choked out what was almost a laugh. Almost. "Quinn, Ty, and Logan."

Cole's eyes widened. Not a lot, but enough that Eve caught it. He pursed his lips as he sat back, his broad shoulders brushing Ren's.

An uncomfortable second of wiggling ensued until a gap grew between them. Maybe touching each other wasn't quite comfortable for them at this moment, during this *situation*. At least, not for Ren. He dropped his head in his hands and she couldn't see his expression. Was he mad? Shocked?

No one wanted to break the silence, as if the first one who did had to explain the reality of the proposal. Of what Eve had just suggested. Even Eve herself didn't know if she was capable of doing it without making more of a mess. This was not her best moment, that was for sure.

But, she knew what she wanted. And what she wanted was both men sitting across from her. That had been her intent all along, but now the reality was sitting right in her lap.

She'd never been so bold in her life. It even surprised her a little bit. But the thought of rejection scared her.

In the past, she had never approached the opposite sex, and had never been so open to what she wanted. She always thought that if a man was interested in her he would approach her. That was what men did. Right?

Maybe. Maybe not. But she had this burning desire deep down inside her she couldn't deny.

Her husband's death proved to her you only live once. Cliché, she knew, but it was true. Why waste time denying what she wanted. What she really desired.

Even if it was only for a little while.

She shrugged mentally. As she kept telling herself, they could always say no…

It could be they weren't as comfortable with each other as she first thought. She believed there might be a connection there… beyond football…beyond friendship. Maybe she was reading it all wrong. Maybe it was simply a bromance. A teammate thing.

She cleared her throat, but before she could speak, Ren stood up, distancing himself from Cole and from her.

Cole stretched his legs out in front of him and leaned back into the couch, looking like the cat that caught the canary. He wore a wide grin. "Everyone knows I've been with men."

Cole had never tried to hide it from his teammates, his fans, or the press. If he was open about it, it removed all the speculation. If you simply handed over the dirt to the public, then it wasn't so exciting anymore. It wasn't a secret. Not that everyone could be so open, Eve thought, but it was so like Cole to be that way. No secrets. No lies.

Here I am, like me or not.

But unless Ren was hiding something, he had never admitted to being anything but a woman-loving male. He appreciated the ladies and the ladies appreciated him. At least for a little while anyway, as rumor had it.

"So have I." The words were soft and almost unheard, since Ren had his back to them. His arms were crossed, and even from behind he looked tense. His shoulders were tight and raised. Yes, maybe just a little tense.

Eve and Cole caught each other's glances. Cole was as clearly surprised as she was. "I was simply curious. I was young."

"That's what they all say," Cole joked.

Ren came behind him on the couch and gently knocked him upside the head. Cole ducked and rubbed his ear, laughing.

"Did you enjoy it?" Cole asked him.

Ren frowned and sat in a chair opposite Eve, but away from Cole. His gaze bore into her as he asked, "So, just to be clear... You want to have a threesome."

"Of course she does."

Ren glared at Cole. "Let her answer."

Eve schooled her expression. "Yes." She sounded calmer than she felt. Imagine that...

"Like on a regular basis. Or just once, only because it's on your bucket list or something, right?"

"Well," she said slowly and in a soothing voice she would use to calm a feral cat. One loud noise and the cat would run away scared. "I'll leave that up to you. I've never done it before. You have to be comfortable with it, too."

"What if I say no? Would you look for someone else?"

Eve's stomach did a flip. Was he actually considering it?

"Ren, I would love it to be you. We have chemistry. At least I thought we did. We've been enjoying each other's company for the past few weeks. And the sex—"

"Has been fucking awesome," he finished. "I know. I know." He groaned. "But, I'm not doing *anything* where there's a possibility of —" Ren crossed his two index fingers together. "Where there's a chance of crossing swords."

"Aren't you secure with your manhood?" Cole asked him.

Cole was doing his best to get a rise out of Ren. Eve rolled her eyes at Cole to let him know he wasn't helping.

Ren snorted. "You know I am. Hell, I just admitted I've had sex with a man before."

"Only once?"

Once again, Ren's answer to Cole was to frown at him.

She watched Ren when she asked tentatively, "So you are both in agreement with this?" She held her breath.

Cole's smile was blinding. "I'm in. I love a good threesome!"

Ren twitched in his chair. Eve released her breath and pinned him with a stare. She pursed her lips and leaned forward. "You don't look so comfortable with this idea."

He tugged on his earring. After a long moment, he stated, "I'm sort of curious."

"Curious." Cole had a smile of triumph plastering his face. "Well, I *am* a sexy, sexy sex machine. I'm hard to resist."

Ren's eyebrows shot up. "You're crazy, Dix. So answer this: Why in the hell would I want to do this?"

Eve settled back in her chair, watching them both. Cole seemed to not only be willing, but willing enough to encourage Ren to try. He was doing all the hard work for her and she was not going to interrupt.

Cole looked like a little boy who was fidgeting with excitement until he was allowed to open presents on Christmas morning. "Baby, you don't know what you're missing."

Ren closed his eyes and took a deep breath. "Now, I know you never forgot to wear your helmet, but you must be fucked up in the head. Especially calling me baby. Just because I got curious in college doesn't mean I'm gay."

Cole spread his hands out. "I'm not gay either."

Ren sighed, clearly impatient. "Okay, *bi*. Close enough, man. Damn."

"I'm open-minded," Cole clarified.

Ren snorted. "Open-minded. Sure." He grimaced. "It's one thing to be open-minded; it's another to be willing to open other *areas*."

"A person has to turn me on. I don't care if it's a he or she, white, black, brown, or yellow. If that person flips my switch, I'm open."

Ren raised his dark brows. "As long as they are open-minded also?"

"Of course, brother. They have to be willing. Who in their right mind doesn't want to be with someone who is willing?"

"And I turn you on?" Ren asked, his pitch a little higher than normal.

It could've been a touchy question, but Cole being Cole just blurted out the answer. "You've always turned me on. You never caught me staring at you in the locker room? Never felt my hands linger a little longer than they should?"

"Fuck!" Ren tapped a finger against his forehead, as if a memory had popped into his head. "You did touch me. You often smacked my ass and squeezed by me."

Cole smiled triumphantly. "I guess that didn't go unnoticed."

"Yeah, you touched me plenty of times. I noticed. But I thought that was just you. Just the way you were. It never bothered me. And I've always known you're bisexual. That didn't bother me either. Otherwise, we wouldn't have been friends this long."

"I was your right-hand man on the field."

Ren's eyes softened as if he was replaying some memories in his head. He relaxed into the chair a little more. "You helped me be a world champion quarterback. We've always worked well together."

"And we could now, too. I know you've had threesomes before, Renny. You've told me about them." Cole was pleading with him as if he finally had that carrot dangling in front of him and he would be so disappointed if Ren said no.

"They were with two women!" He shot a look over at Eve and she schooled her face to be blank. Of course he'd had threesomes before. That didn't bother her. Just as she was as sure Cole had. If someone was to poll the room on who *hadn't* had a threesome, she'd be the only one raising her hand. And tonight she was going to go big or go home.

"It's not much different with two guys. We could keep Eve between us. It's not like I'm going to accidentally slip inside you, like 'whoops, sorry, wrong hole.'"

Ren fought back a grin. "You're not making this any easier."

"It's not a difficult thing, Renny. It's really not. You're just getting inside your own head. How about this… We try it. You can fuck Eve, and I'll simply watch. Or I can just play with Eve a little bit while you're fucking her. I won't purposely touch you unless you say it's okay. Just keep an open mind. That's all I ask."

"Wait. Were you in on this from the get-go? Did you and Eve plan this all along?"

Eve finally spoke. "No, it was all mine. Like I said, I envy what Quinn has with her lovers. I would love to have that with you two. Cole had no idea."

"Renny, if she would have told me, I still would've shown up today."

If Eve would have known Cole would be this enthused about the whole idea, she would have confessed her plan to him a couple weeks ago. "Look, we have this house for the weekend. Or longer, if we want it. Let's just enjoy it. No pressure."

Cole nodded, "Let's just enjoy each other."

Enjoy each other's company, each other's bodies, each other's pleasure… It sounded good to Eve. And clearly also to Cole. Then after the weekend? See where it leads, if anywhere. But it would go nowhere if Ren wasn't willing to explore their connection first.

The right thing to do at this point was to give Ren some space. Let him mull it over.

"I have stuff in the fridge to make dinner. I have some beer and wine chilling. We could just relax for a while." she suggested. "Let Ren absorb my…" Proposal? Suggestion? "Idea."

"Well, I, for one, vote for a weekend of complete debauchery!"

Eve laughed at Cole, but she watched Ren. His expression was pensive. Maybe he was considering everything that was said?

Oh boy, she hoped so. A shiver ran through her and she gave him a smile.

CHAPTER 9

Cole sat in the deck chair, legs stretched out, listening to the waves crash just beyond them in the dark. They had turned off the lights in the house so they could see the stars. It was a clear night, the breeze a little chilly.

During and after dinner, no one mentioned the threesome. But Cole couldn't stop thinking about it. He was sure everyone was thinking about it, because no one was talking. Instead, they were drinking their second bottle of a semi-sweet red wine. Ren was hitting it a little harder than either Cole or Eve, but maybe he was merely trying to calm his nerves.

Cole broke the easy silence. "I have a plan."

Both heads rotated in unison toward him, almost as if he was breaking some rule of silence.

"Or maybe more of a suggestion…if you both are willing." He gazed out into the darkness, ignoring their stares. "Or maybe it's a want."

"Fucking Dix! Just say it."

The frustration in Ren's voice made him look his way.

"Okay, I want to fuck Eve while you watch."

The testosterone in the air ratcheted up a level. "Why can't I fuck Eve while *you* watch?"

"Hear me out. You watch us and when…*if* you want to join in, you do it when you're comfortable." The silence stretched until Cole turned to Eve. "Are you okay with that?"

"Sure, if Ren is." She took a sip, more like a gulp, of wine. Apparently, Ren wasn't the only one fighting nerves.

Ren snagged the bottle of wine from where it sat beside Eve's feet. He emptied the remainder into his glass and guzzled it.

"Why don't you just drink straight out of the bottle?" Cole frowned.

Ren shot him a look, then wiped his mouth with the back of his hand. Cole watched him move through the open glass doors to the kitchen, pull a fresh bottle out of the wine cooler, uncork it, and drink straight from the bottle.

Unfortunately, Ren had taken his teasing seriously.

Cole gave Eve a look and tipped his chin toward Ren. She only nodded, concern crossing her face.

Ren came back out on the deck, standing between Cole and Eve, the now half-empty bottle dangling from his fingers. Ren was not a big drinker, so if he had to fortify himself this much with alcohol…

"Brother, you could always say no."

"I don't want to…say no. Let's do this."

Cole looked up in surprise at the man he'd desired for so long. The man he thought he'd never have. His broad but chiseled face, the short hair—which he now preferred over his former cornrows. His deep expressive eyes, those wide, kissable lips, muscles well-honed and powerful. Ren was bulked up more now than when he was playing football. Many times, they had worked out together, Cole watching, out of the corner of his eye, the ripple of Ren's muscles as he worked them hard with weights. And he had seen his best friend naked plenty enough to know what was hanging downstairs. If Ren ever wanted to top him, Cole would have to make sure he was prepared. Well prepared.

He realized his mouth was hanging open. He closed it and cleared his throat.

"Now," Ren stated. He helped Eve out of her chair and led her back into the house.

Cole sat for a second longer, making sure he just heard what he heard. He pinched himself. Yep, he was awake. Then he stood so quickly the Adirondack chair he was lounging in tipped back and over, crashing to the deck.

Fuck. This was going to happen!

He pulled at his shorts, adjusting his hard-on. He rushed into the house, his heart beating crazily. He dug through his duffle bag, which was still lying by the front door, and found condoms and Astroglide.

When he entered the master bedroom, Ren and Eve stood there, a strip of condoms in each of their hands.

Eve gave a nervous laugh. "I guess we all came prepared."

Cole threw his supplies on the nightstand and stripped off his shirt, tossing it haphazardly. He stumbled when he tried to pull his shorts off too quickly. His cock was already hard and kept catching in the fabric of his boxer briefs as he finally tugged them off.

He turned in all his fully naked glory, and realized Eve and Ren were still both fully clothed and watching him. He felt like a virgin about to get his cherry popped. "What. Can't a man be anxious for what's about to happen?"

Ren just shook his head, threw his condoms on top of Cole's, and settled into an upholstered chair facing the bed.

Cole moved over to Eve, who stood there with a deer-in-the-headlights expression. He realized if he didn't control his own eagerness, this might turn into a complete fail. He needed to keep his head on straight to assure Eve, to make her feel comfortable. He gave her a soothing smile as he removed the condoms from her clenched fist and tossed them onto the bed. He turned her so she faced Ren where he was sitting, watching. The wine bottle now three-quarters empty by his feet.

"Relax," Cole murmured against her ear. He ran his tongue around the edge of it. "You wanted this. It's happening." He sucked on her earlobe before moving to her mouth. He brushed his lips over hers. "I want you naked," he whispered against her mouth, his fingers grabbing the hem of her shirt and pulling it up until her bra was exposed. His fingers brushed along the lace, over the upper curve of her breasts, dipping into her cleavage. "That would be a perfect place for my cock when he's fucking you."

Eve's sigh brushed his cheek, and he stepped back to finish pulling the shirt over her head. He moved behind her to unhook her bra, and caught her breasts in his hands when the bra fell to the floor. He held the soft weight of them in his palms, his thumbs brushing lightly over her tight nipples.

Cole felt her shiver as he squeezed one breast, his other hand sliding down her stomach until he traced the waist of her shorts. He popped the button and unzipped them slowly, occasionally peeking at Ren nonchalantly, trying to read his reaction.

Ren's expression was tight, but Cole could see the flare of his nostrils. He was fighting it. He only hoped that Ren's struggle with himself wasn't a fight to keep from running out of the room, that Ren watching him undress Eve was turning him on. Cole needed to turn it up a notch. Or two.

He wanted to make sure Ren felt pulled in and not pushed away.

Cole slid his hand into her shorts and under her panties to find the dampness, the warmth he craved. He stroked a finger between her folds, and she gasped, slamming her head back into his chest. He placed his lips on the curve of her neck, licked, and nibbled, making her quiver and groan.

He slid his slick finger along her folds once again, brushing her clit. "You're so wet. I'm going to fuck you so good. I'm going to fuck you until you come all over me." He slipped a finger inside her and then a second. She thrust her hips back against him. His cock was sandwiched between them, pulsing, his balls tight. "Take off your shorts and panties."

She released the back of his head where she had gripped him fiercely, to yank off her shorts and her panties in one movement. They landed around her ankles. His fingers never left her cunt, and her body clenched around them. Now Ren could see everything Cole did to Eve. He could watch every response her body made. He couldn't miss the way her knees buckled a bit, the movement of her hips against his hand, her closed eyes, her open mouth, her ragged breathing.

But Ren still sat there, unmoving, his eyes slightly hooded and dark. His fingers gripped the wooden arms of the chair.

Cole picked Eve up and placed her on the bed. Her head landed on the pillow, her eyes remained unfocused. He slid beside her, careful not to block Ren's view.

He slid his fingers into her again, sucking one nipple, then the other. She was warm and tight, and so damn wet. With each thrust of his fingers, she made little sounds, encouraging him to speed up, to get a little rougher.

He bit the soft curve of her breast over one nipple and she cried out.

"Oh, fuck me."

It was a plea he found hard to resist. His cock was so hard against her hip. She reached out to grab the crown of his cock, but he shifted enough to stay out of her reach. He could only take so much.

"Soon. I want to taste you first."

She hissed a "Yes." Eve wanted—no, needed—his mouth on her. Her body was humming.

Cole pushed himself down the bed a little more and settled between her thighs, guiding her knees over his shoulders, completely exposing her pussy to him.

His fingers separating her plump lips, as if he were looking for treasure. After a last stroke of his fingers through her slickness, his mouth replaced them.

His tongue traced the edge of every fold, pausing on her

sensitive clit. Sucking lightly, then harder. One flick with his tongue, then another, over and over until her head flung back into the pillow. Her eyes rolled back and she tilted her hips, trying not to grind against his mouth. But it was hard not to. So hard. She wanted to come. She needed to come.

She wanted him to fuck her. *Now.*

His tongue dipped in and out of her, but it wasn't enough. His tongue was quickly replaced once again by a finger, then two. His mouth was back on her clit as he sucked, all the while his fingers plunging in and out. She was hot and wet and open to him. Her body was more than ready for him.

He crooked his fingers and found the spot. He stroked her until she felt like she would bloom like a flower. Her hands had a death grip on the sheets as she mewed her pleasure. Hot lightning shot down her legs, curling her toes, then shot back up, landing in her center. She cried out as her core pulsed intensely around his fingers. But he didn't let up.

Her clit was so sensitive to touch from the orgasm that she cried out, almost painfully, as he continued to explore her swollen lips and everything in between.

"Stop. Stop!" she cried out.

He stilled and lifted his head. His smoky green eyes met hers. The smile on his face was proof enough he enjoyed this as much as she did.

She had a fleeting thought about whether he was enjoying it even more because Ren was watching them.

"No more?"

"I can't," she said breathlessly.

"That was only the beginning," he promised, with a slight head tilt toward the quiet Ren.

"I know!" She tried to laugh, but couldn't catch her breath enough to. Not only was she breathless but she felt boneless. If one man could do this to her, what was going to happen when there were two?

He moved up her body until his hips were settled between her thighs. Both warm hardness and softness pressed against her, his shaft against her still sensitive mound.

He kissed her breasts lightly. When she arched her back, he nibbled around each nipple. They were painfully hard, but even then, she was desperate for his touch, his mouth. He sucked one into his mouth, rolling it around with his tongue, tasting and teasing. His thumb and forefinger captured the other, rolling the hard nub between his fingers, then stretching and pulling on it.

Shockwaves landed in her belly and lower. "Cole, Cole…don't tease me."

Cole gave her a wicked smile. "Put a condom on me."

Eve felt around for the string of condoms he had thrown on the bed and ripped one off and open. She slid it over his hard length, lingering, fingers brushing.

With hooded eyes, Cole's jaw tightened as she released him. He rolled her onto her stomach and yanked her hips up and back toward him. He bent down and gently bit into the soft roundness of her ass. Eve loved when he bit her. It was gentle enough that it didn't hurt badly, but hard enough to bring all the endorphins rushing through her system. It made her nipples tighten painfully and her pussy feel like it was dripping. She'd be surprised if there wasn't a wet puddle under her.

He tested her slickness with his thumb. "So wet. I want to sink myself deep inside you."

She muffled a frustrated scream into the sheets. "Do it!"

Her pussy pulsated, waiting and wanting to feel the head of his cock at her opening. Instead, he slid his thumb through her wetness one more time, then pressed it against her anus, not quite breaking through, but putting pressure where she wasn't used to. But before she could give it too much thought, he pushed his cock into her. Deep. So deep. Her insides stretched to accommodate his girth, his length. He filled her up tight. His ragged breath blew across her heated skin. He blew another.

He slowly slid out of her completely. She felt empty, wanting. She wanted him to fuck her hard. To give her all he had, all he could give her. And then even more.

He pushed back into her slowly, and when he reached her limit, his thumb slipped into her ass, stretching her there too. A whimper escaped her as he took up a rhythm with his thumb to match his hips. He slid in and out of her, in and out. The sensation was unfamiliar to her, but she closed her eyes, and gave him access to all of her. Her pussy, her ass. He was taking it all as his.

"I'm going to fuck you in the ass."

"No," she groaned. She couldn't take his size there. It was impossible.

"Yes. Not tonight, but soon. I'll have you begging for it."

His thumb pushed deeper until he was knuckle deep. His hips moved against her faster, harder. He reached around her with his free hand, balancing all his weight on his knees. He found her clit with his middle finger, stroking, pushing, tweaking.

The rhythm of his thumb, his middle finger, and his cock synchronized. Each touch, each sensation bringing her closer to the edge. She gripped the sheets in her fists, and cried into the mattress with each thrust. His cock pulsated inside her as he stroked her spot, the spot that wanted to make her break open and lose herself all over the bed. All over Cole.

"I'm going to come," she cried out. His rhythm got more intense, more frantic. He pinched her clit between his thumb and forefinger.

She cursed and cried as the waves of orgasm rippled through her body, from her core to her toes and back up again. The throbbing of her pussy matched the thumping of her heart. And he didn't stop. He pounded into her, their skin smacking together. He released her clit and her ass to grab her hips, to pound her harder. And again, the waves broke over her, through her. Her inner walls clenched him so tight it made him cry out her name and still, the base of his cock pulsating as he released deep inside her.

Ren's cock was so hard he swore he was going to have blue balls when this was all over.

He had released the button and zipper on his shorts after Cole put Eve on the bed. And now, his trembling hand was squeezing the base, smoothing along his length, the thick vein pulsating underneath his fingers. He reversed his grip and stroked himself while Cole fucked Eve, making her writhe and scream. He had done that to her also. It should be him between her thighs, fucking her until she came. But it wasn't.

He watched Cole's ass flex and push as he fucked Eve from behind with his cock, playing with her, fucking her ass with his thumb.

He couldn't turn away. He couldn't do anything but watch. And he realized he wanted to, he was so turned on by Cole fucking Eve. He wasn't jealous. He was envious, he should have joined them sooner.

Shit.

Ren had enough. He couldn't sit there and watch Cole pleasure Eve anymore, watch her writhe and cry out under his friend, dig her nails into Cole's back. He stood suddenly, the chair he was sitting in sliding back and banging against the wall.

But by then Cole had stilled and then collapsed beside Eve, who slid to her belly, breathless.

They both turned at the bang.

"Let me tell you something…" He moved next to the bed, studying their naked bodies, their limbs intertwined. "That was some of the hottest shit I've ever seen." He stepped closer. Close enough he could touch them. "I'm so freaking hard right now."

Cole sat up to extend out his hand in invitation. "Well, come on then. Let us help you with your dilemma."

Ren put a knee on the bed, the mattress sinking with his weight. "I don't know…"

"Yes, you do. I won't touch you if you don't want. You can do all the touching," Cole reassured him. "But…will you be okay with accidental touching?"

Ren's first instinct was to say no, but Cole had asked him to stay open-minded and he told himself he would. "Fine. I can live with *accidental* touching."

"If I do something by *accident* that makes you uncomfortable, just say something."

Ren frowned. "Like a safe word?"

Cole laughed. "No, you don't need a safe word. Simply point out what I'm doing. I might not even realize it. I want you to be comfortable, but I also want to expand your boundaries."

"I think I'm worried about the *expanding* part."

"I want us *all* to enjoy it. No one to feel left out," Eve added, a sparkle in her eyes. She was clearly excited about the prospect of Ren joining them, her nervousness from earlier gone now.

"You'll be the cream in our cookie sandwich."

Eve smiled at Cole. "That's all I can ask for!"

"Do you want Eve to undress you?" Cole asked him.

Ren shook his head. As tight as his balls were, as hard as his cock was, having Eve undress him might be his undoing. If he was going to lose his load, he wanted to be doing something other than undressing.

He pulled his shirt over his head and threw it. His shorts were already undone, the engorged head of his cock peeking out of the top of his boxer briefs. He peeled out of his shorts and briefs and threw them out of the way, too.

He stood naked in front of Cole, his curved hard length touching his belly. They had seen each other naked a million times before. There was no shyness to be had in the locker rooms and showers before and after games and practices. But never had they seen each other hard, aroused.

However, tonight was different.

Cole moved back to lean against the headboard, Eve on her side practically curled around him.

Cole studied Ren's body slowly from head to foot. Ren thought that would make him lose his erection. It didn't. His cock twitched under the other man's gaze.

Eve uncurled herself from Cole and moved away, patting the bed between them. Cole shifted a little, giving him space.

Ren stared at the spot Eve patted, the spot they'd made for him.

He cautiously climbed up in between. Cole, keeping his word, didn't touch him, but he didn't move away either. They sat shoulder to shoulder against the headboard.

Eve crawled into his lap and straddled his hips. Her wet heat against his balls, his cock sandwiched between them. Precum was gathering at the tip. Eve ran a thumb over it, swirling it over the head, down his length. He thrust into her hand, losing the little control he was fighting for.

Eve met his gaze. She smiled, then leaned forward to kiss him, her hands braced against his pecs. She skimmed his nipples with her palms.

She kissed him along his neck, over his shoulder, down his chest. As she did so, she moved between his legs, brushing her lips over his belly, along his hip. She placed her lips on the inside of his thighs, and nibbled along his skin. She took his sac into her mouth, her tongue rolling his balls around.

Holy fuck.

He couldn't get any harder; he couldn't wait to be deep inside her anymore.

Her fingers replaced her mouth. She cupped his balls as she licked the crown of his cock. Around and down and back up again, capturing the precum on her tongue.

He groaned, leaning his head back against the headboard. He closed his eyes, enjoying the feel of her tongue and her lips.

The mattress shifted as Eve moved down to take his length in her mouth.

Oh, fuck. Her mouth was so hot and wet. She sucked him deep again and again. In the few weeks they had been seeing each other, she'd never taken him this deep before. He fought to keep from thrusting up into her mouth, down her throat.

He was so close. Oh God, he wanted to fuck her, but he couldn't move. He wanted this. He wanted to come down her throat. Her hand squeezed the root, keeping him from coming for a moment, making the pleasure last.

He reached down to grab a handful of her long silky hair. His fingers encountered a smooth, bald head instead. His eyes flew open.

What the fuck!

He grabbed Cole's skull and before he could push him off, Cole mumbled "Relax" around his hard cock.

Holy hell! How was that cocksucker so good at...sucking his cock? Why wasn't he losing his erection?

He should be fighting him off, pushing him away.

But he couldn't. He couldn't.

Eve was on her back under Cole, sucking the other man's cock at the same time. They had tricked him. They'd swapped places. But *damn...*

Cole took him deep into his mouth. He could almost deep throat Ren's whole length. Impressive.

"Ah, fuck."

Cole paused at the top. "Do you want me to stop?

"Yes. No. Fuck, I'm about to come."

Cole smiled before continuing. It was *his* hand wrapped around the base of him. *His* hand squeezing him as he sucked him. *His* hand cupping his balls.

Ren looked past him to what Eve was doing. She was sucking Cole as hard as Cole was sucking him. Cole was on his knees, giving Eve room in between them. She had her fingers circled around Cole's balls, which were becoming a dark purple. She rolled her eyes up toward Ren and smiled around Cole's hard length. She reached her free hand down between her legs and played with herself. Ren couldn't quite see what she was doing, but he could imagine.

What he imagined was enough to make him stiffen and flex his toes, warning Cole, "I'm coming!"

Cole kept sucking him, taking Ren's load down his throat. He didn't stop until Ren was depleted and weak. Cole released him and laid his head on Ren's thigh, moaning as Eve continued to stroke him over and over with her mouth and squeeze his balls. Finally, Eve let his sac go, the normal color returning slowly, and Cole tensed, grabbing at the sheets on either side of Ren.

"Oh fuck," Cole cried out against Ren's skin. "Oh fuck!"

Ren placed a hand on Cole's back. He was warm, his skin damp under his palm. "I want to see you come in her mouth."

Ren watched the muscles of Cole's ass clench as he cried out, coming.

Cole relaxed against him, lying on Ren's legs as Eve rolled out from underneath him, catching her breath.

She dragged herself up beside Ren, curling under his arm, nuzzling his neck.

"Are you okay?" he asked her.

"Perfect," she answered, and smiled at him. "Thank you."

"For what?"

"For this. For even considering it."

Ren didn't answer her but looked at Cole, still sprawled over his legs. His breathing was slow and soft, tickling Ren's balls, his mouth barely an inch away.

If he hadn't just come, Ren would be hard again. Cole's cock was now soft against Ren's calf.

He shook himself mentally. What was he thinking? He wasn't gay! He wasn't attracted to men!

He never had any sexual desire for Cole before. Yes, he loved him as a brother, a friend. That was normal, right?

But Cole had sucked him until he came. He had better skills than any woman he'd been with, even Eve. He probably had more practice.

But what bothered Ren the most was he had liked it. *He liked it.*

And knowing Eve had been pleasuring Cole as he was pleasuring Ren made it that much hotter.

Damn it!

Ren kicked Cole with his foot.

"Ow!"

He scowled at Cole. "Don't you ever do that again!" Ren added, "Especially, without asking me first!"

Cole gave him a wide smile. "Okay, but you'll be asking."

Ren grimaced. Cole was not only a good cocksucker, but a cocky one too.

CHAPTER 10

Not long after Cole teased Ren about how he'd be asking Cole to suck his cock again, Ren peeled himself out of the puppy pile they were lying in. He gathered his clothes and walked out of the bedroom. Not a word spoken, not a backward glance.

Eve was going to follow him to talk to him, but Cole stopped her. "Just let him be for now, let him process."

She nodded her head, sighed resignedly, and climbed back into bed with Cole. They had snuggled until they fell asleep, which didn't take long at all. Her last words to him were her hoping Ren would return and she'd wake up between the two of them.

But this morning Ren was nowhere to be found. None of the spare beds had been slept in. His overnight bag with his clothes was gone.

Both Eve and Cole had tried to call and text him. They got no response.

Cole could see the worry on Eve's face as she moved around the bright kitchen. She tugged at her lower lip with her teeth, not even realizing she was doing it.

Cole moved up behind her to hug her. He wanted to reassure her that Ren's disappearance wasn't her doing. She stiffened at first, but after a moment she sank against him. He ran his hands over her shoulders, down to her fingertips, and back up again.

"What did I do, Cole? This is all my fault."

"Nothing. It was me. I pushed him. I shouldn't have tricked him like that." He frowned into Eve's hair, smelling the fruity scent of her shampoo. He loved to feel her hair all over him when he was naked.

"I hope he's okay."

"He'll be fine. He's a big boy. He can take care of himself."

"But—"

He cut her short, trying to get her mind off what happened. "I'm hungry. What's to eat?"

"I thought about making Belgian waffles with fresh strawberries."

"That sounds good, but I was thinking of something else first. A little appetizer."

She leaned back against him, turning her head slightly. "What?"

Cole pushed the long T-shirt she was wearing up above the swell of her hips and palmed her soft mound over top of her little pink panties. "This."

His arms pinned her around the waist from behind as he reached with one hand to pull aside the cotton panties. He stroked her warm pussy with his other hand. She must have shaved in the shower this morning. Her lips were super smooth where he touched them. He slid two fingers into her warm canal.

"Not so wet this morning?" Cole murmured against her ear. Her chest heaved and she squeezed her body around his fingers. He fucked her slowly, feeling the clench and unclench of her muscles. "Ah, there it is. Drench my hand." She grasped the edge of the counter as he worked his way in and out of her. Her head fell forward, her hair hiding her face. "That's it. You're so wet now. Just how I like it. That's it, baby." Her muscles clamped tight. "Fuck, yes."

Cole's hard-on pressed through the thin cotton of the T-shirt, pushing against the crease between her ass cheeks. Her hips rocked against his fingers, which made him rock against her ass.

"I'm going to pinch your clit and you're going to come, okay?" His voice was low and rough even to his own ears.

"Oooo…kay," she whispered.

He slid his ring finger and pinky finger inside her and used his thumb and index finger to snag her clit and squeeze.

Eve cried out and her knees buckled. He wrapped his arm across her chest, above her breasts, holding her up and against him. He could bend her over right there against the counter and drive it home. It wouldn't take much to feel her wet heat around his throbbing cock. But… not yet.

"Did you like that?"

She nodded, breathing hard.

He turned her around and kissed her hard, his lips pressing against hers, his tongue forcing them open so he could explore her mouth. He captured her moan between his lips.

He swung her up into his arms and laid her on the kitchen table, her ass at the edge, her legs dangling over. Her shirt was pushed up to her breasts, exposing her hard peaks. He wanted to bite them hard. He wanted to hear her cry out. He wanted to leave teeth marks in the sensitive flesh around her nipples. Patience. Patience, he told himself.

He snagged her panties and tugged them off. Dropping to his knees, he was at the right height. He pressed her thighs apart. Her pussy was beautiful. Pink, smooth, and shiny from her orgasm. He didn't know if he'd ever been with a woman who got so wet, whose juices gushed out of her when she came. All over his cock, or his fingers, or his mouth…

At that thought he pressed his mouth to her, licking her, tasting her, inhaling the scent of her all excited and ready.

He spread her wider with his fingers and he buried his face against her, stroking her with his tongue, sucking her clit. He pinned her hips down with his arm to keep her from bucking against the table.

"Now this is my kind of breakfast," he said before burying himself between her legs once again.

She let out a long wail and her hips fought against the weight of his arm. He felt a warm gush against his lips, his face, before he pulled back with a smile. He wiped the back of his hand over his mouth and stood.

Her pussy was ripe and ready for him to fuck her good, fuck her hard. Fuck her until she came over and over, drenching his cock and his balls.

"I'm going to fuck you now," he told her, stripping out of his clothes, throwing them onto a chair, which he had impatiently shoved away from the kitchen table.

"Yes," she moaned. "Yes."

He cursed himself when he realized he didn't have a condom. As he turned, a rush of air hit him and all the oxygen left his lungs as he was body slammed. He stumbled back, trying to catch his breath and his balance. Eve scrambled off the table and yelled at Ren.

"Ren! Stop!"

Cole heard the panic in her voice, but he fought the urge to defend himself. Ren wouldn't hurt him. Not really. He was pissed off, that's all. They were like brothers.

Ren grabbed him by the shoulders, shoving him face down onto the table. Cole grunted as his teeth cut his lip.

Ren kicked Cole's feet wide as he kept him pinned to the kitchen table. Cole felt nothing but empty space behind him, then the unmistakable sound of a zipper. Ren shifted a hand to the back of Cole's neck, while the other was on his cock, finding Cole's tight hole.

Ren was going to fuck him. He was right there, the broad head of his cock pressing against the tight entrance. Cole's mind spun.

"Lube," Cole groaned out. When Ren didn't move, didn't shift his cock away from his opening, he added, "Please!"

Ren still didn't move. Ren stood, breathing hard, holding Cole down. His ass was completely exposed but Ren still stood frozen... as if his brain had just caught up to what he was about to do, the reality of it all.

From the corner of his eye, Cole saw Eve rush out of the kitchen and back, shoving a bottle of Astroglide and a condom at Ren.

The rip of the wrapper and the snap of the bottle being opened made a shiver run down Cole's spine.

Ren wasn't going to be gentle. Oh no. He was angry and upset. Cole could only imagine that Ren had stewed for hours and wanted to take out all the feelings that had been flayed open last night out on Cole. Was Ren blaming Cole for his bisexual desires? Ones he didn't want to admit?

Clearly, Ren was out to punish Cole.

For tempting him? For pushing the other man far enough that he was going to fuck Cole right in the kitchen where the morning light exposed all his secrets.

Cole couldn't see Ren's face, but he felt the press of Ren's thick, hard cock at his anus; Ren's fingers digging tightly into the back of his neck with more strength than was needed.

Cole had no desire to fight. No need to flee. He would bear the brunt of Ren's anger, at least this time. He understood the raw feelings Ren felt. He had known them himself way back when. Back when he'd discovered his own true sexuality.

With a curse, Ren thrust inside him. Not working his way in slowly, gently stretching Cole's canal to fit him. No, Ren was going to fuck him without mercy. Cole could only wonder if the other man was going to fuck him this roughly to prove he was still in control. Maybe Ren thought he had lost a bit of his masculinity last night and needed to show Cole who was still dominant, who was all male.

Whatever the reason, Cole could feel each emotion with Ren's every thrust. Anger. Frustration. Fear.

Ren pounded him.

Cole had wanted him for a long time but had never told anyone. He had kept quiet because he'd never thought it would happen. Well, thanks to Eve, it was happening. Maybe not quite like he'd envisioned, but he hoped it would get there. That Ren would want him as much as Cole wanted Ren.

But for now, he would take what he could get. And at the moment, he was getting a good ass reaming. His body rocked hard against the wooden table each time Ren thrust. With each slam Cole groaned and Ren grunted.

He stayed as relaxed as he could, even though Ren still held him down forcefully.

The rhythmic slap of Ren's hips against his ass made him close his eyes to concentrate on his movements, on each grunt Ren released.

Cole jerked in surprise when a hand grabbed his partially erect cock. From under the kitchen table, Eve stroked him and then swallowed him deep.

He fought to concentrate on Eve's mouth as she gripped the base of his cock and sucked him, licked him, nibbled along his shaft. She kept him hard, ready, and it confused his body. The pleasure from the front, the punishment from the back.

Suddenly, Ren skipped a beat, slowed, his breathing heavy. Unexpectedly, Ren released Cole's neck to grip Cole's hips tightly with his fingers.

Cole finally had enough freedom to tilt his pelvis, to meet Ren's thrusts, to make the angle more pleasurable. Eve was trying to keep the same rhythm with her mouth along his cock, licking the length, taking it deep into her mouth.

Ren's rhythm became frantic again and Ren cried out, spilling himself deep inside Cole.

Cole moaned as Ren's cock pulsated deep in his canal.

Eve picked up speed, and Cole cried out as he released himself, Eve's throat working to get every drop of his come. She let him slide out of her mouth and she kissed the still engorged head before crawling out from underneath the table.

Ren was still, his breathing a bit quick. He dropped his forehead to let it rest on Cole's back. Cole felt Ren's hot breath blow along his warm, damp skin.

Eve got to her feet and moved behind Ren, leaning against his back, wrapping her arms as much as she could around both men, trying to hold them both close. She rested her cheek against Ren's back.

She was desperate not to cry, to bring Ren's torment back to the surface. But her heart was breaking.

She whispered, "Sorry."

She didn't know if she was apologizing to one, the other, or both. All of them. She was sorry it had come to this. She was sorry she had come up with this plan in the first place. She was sorry Cole had to take the punishment he had just taken, even though he accepted it without a complaint. She was sorry to Ren for pushing him to the point of breaking. For making him stir up desires he never wanted to bring to the surface.

"Eve. You have to move. I'm crushing Cole." Ren's voice sounded tired and defeated.

She moved away, giving them space. Ren offered a hand to Cole, who accepted it, even gripped it tightly as Ren pulled him to his feet.

As soon as Cole was standing, he found his shorts, pulling them back up his hips. Ren ripped off the condom and chucked it into the garbage with more force than was necessary, his face revealing nothing.

But Eve had seen a flash of something before his expression had become blank. Something was simmering. Regret?

Most likely. He had been rough on Cole. And Cole was his closest friend.

Ren straightened his camo cargo pants and fastened them closed before turning to face them.

He kept his eyes averted from Cole, but he rasped, "What the fuck did I do? I'm sorry, Dix."

"We are brothers for life, Renny. Don't be sorry."

"I wanted to do it."

"So you're mad that you wanted to fuck me?"

"Fuck yes! And dammit! I..." His fists clenched. "I liked it!"

Cole shook his head and forced a laugh. "I liked it, too. Well, I might not have liked it so much if Eve hadn't gotten the lube. Or sucked me off. But that's not important..."

"Did I hurt you?"

"No, so don't stress yourself out over this, brother."

"I wouldn't blame you if you never forgave me."

Cole brushed a kiss against Eve's check, whispering, "Thanks for the lube." To Ren, he said louder, "Nothing to forgive."

Cole filled the coffeemaker with water and ground coffee and turned it on. Eve watched him act as if nothing was wrong, nothing had happened between the two men.

"Bullshit," Ren exclaimed loudly.

Eve thought Ren might beat himself up over this for a long time. She hoped not. Cole wasn't holding it against him. Ren should let it go and move on.

"Next time—"

"Next time?" Ren barked. He turned away, but Eve felt the urge to touch him. To soothe him. So she took him into her arms. He tensed. He was closed off, but he didn't pull away.

"Next time we'll be better prepared," she said to him quietly.

Ren scowled at her. "I just fucked my best friend in the ass. I'm not sure if I could ever be prepared for that."

Cole chuckled. Eve raised her eyebrows at Cole. She didn't think Ren found any of this funny.

But whether she liked it or not, Cole ignored her silent plea. "Renny, you don't have to fit yourself into a neat little box. It doesn't matter what label you *think* you have to wear. Whether you are hetero, bi-sexual, bi-curious, or even heteroflexible, neither Eve nor I care. Hell, make up your own term. Just be *you*."

The coffeemaker beeped and Cole dug out three mugs. He filled them and held one out to Ren. Black. Ren liked his coffee black. She had spent the night at his house more than a couple times in the last few weeks. She was only beginning to learn about Ren's likes and habits. But Cole knew. Cole knew so much about the man he'd been friends with for a long time and finally admitted out in the open yesterday he'd wanted for a while, but had done nothing about.

As Ren accepted the mug, Cole's fingers brushed along the other man's. Obviously not accidentally. "I've wanted to touch you for a long time. I've wanted to show you pleasure like you've never had before. And I still do."

Ren took a sip of the hot coffee and moved to lean against the kitchen counter. "All these years and you never said anything."

"Of course, you never told me that you were with men—or a *man*, whatever—in college. Until yesterday, at least. If I had known, I would've suggested us experimenting sooner."

Ren's brows furrowed. "I thought we were friends…*best* friends."

Cole sighed; he took his own coffee and leaned against the frame of one of the open sliding glass doors. He probably wasn't in any condition to sit, Eve thought.

"Right. And a best friend would've told me that you experimented in college. Baby, it's not like I want to marry you, I just want to fuck you. Or you fuck me."

Ren grimaced. "Please don't call me baby."

Cole waved his free hand through the air. "Fine, *Renny*. I'll call Eve baby. She probably won't mind. Right, Eve?"

Eve nodded her agreement, but kept moving around the kitchen, gathering ingredients for breakfast. She would let the two men figure things out. At this point, her input was not needed, and maybe not even wanted. She was fine with that.

Cole continued, "If you're not comfortable with," he waved his hand again, "all of this, then fine, stop. But if it's something you think you will enjoy and don't want to admit it to yourself, just give yourself a break. Explore what you want. Eve's open to it. I'm definitely open to it. Some people want a neat label. Fucking life isn't neat. It's messy. For that, I'm glad. I like messy. I don't want to be put into a box. Fuck boxes."

Eve dug out the ingredients for the waffles and started to mix them, keeping a careful ear on their conversation. If she needed to interrupt, or even break the two of them apart, she would.

"Fuck boxes? Maybe that's easy for you. But what about—"

Cole must have known where Ren was going, because Eve was surprised when he cut the larger man off.

"No one needs to know but us. Eve's not going to spill the beans, and you know I won't. I don't need to walk out in public with you on my arm. This is our personal life. No one needs to know shit. It'll all be up to you on how you ride this roller coaster. No pressure."

She fussed with the waffle iron before going back to whipping the batter. She heard nothing behind her. The silence grew. Eve turned her head to check on them, to make sure Ren wasn't strangling the shit out of Cole.

What she saw made her drop the whisk. It clattered onto the counter, the batter spattering all over the counter and floor, all over her.

They were in each other's arms, not strangling, but hugging. She wasn't sure if it was a passionate hug or simply a "buddy" hug. But she'd take it either way.

She could see Ren's face from where she stood.

A flash of heat, a flair of passion crossed Ren's expression, filled his eyes. Something dark and forbidden. But as quickly as it came, it was hidden by his hooded gaze. Almost as if he had been surprised by his reaction and didn't want either of them to know.

Eve realized he wasn't against this at all. But he was fighting his reaction; he didn't want to seem eager.

"I'm sorry, Dix. I never meant to hurt you," Ren mumbled.

"We've already had this discussion. You didn't. Now kiss me and make it all better."

Ren snorted and pushed Cole away. He took his coffee over to the table and settled in one of the chairs. He gave Eve a look.

"When are the waffles going to be ready?"

Eve turned back to clean up the mess, smiling to herself.

CHAPTER 11

In the late afternoon, Cole went out for a run on the beach, leaving Ren and Eve alone at the house.

Ren was sitting in one of the deck chairs when Eve came out, handing him a beer. Ren caught her fingers and pulled her into his lap.

Eve settled against him with a long sigh. "I wish the water was warmer. I'd love to go for a swim."

"I wish I knew how to swim."

Eve turned to look at him in surprise. She searched his face. "You're kidding, right?"

He lifted a shoulder and pointed to himself. "Inner-city kid. We didn't have a lot of opportunities to learn."

"They didn't have any swimming programs where you grew up? YMCAs?" She leaned back against him, the warm sun on her face, his warm chest spooning her back.

"They cost money." He leaned a cheek on the top of her head. "My moms wanted me to play football. She wanted me to get a scholarship to go to college. Her ultimate goal was for me to go pro. So, she dragged me around to football practices whenever she could. She burned whatever little money she had on what she thought was priority. I think I started playing around five, believe it or not."

"What about your dad?"

He traced his fingers along her shoulders and kissed the back of her neck. "No dad."

"Everybody has a dad."

"No. Everybody has a birth father—a sperm donor. Not every father is a dad."

"You never met him?"

"No."

"Did you ever want to?"

"No. I thought once I became pro, he'd come crawling out of the woodwork to collect some of the glory. Not to mention the money. But he didn't. My moms said he probably forgot who she was and never would put two and two together."

"Why do you say 'moms'?"

"Old habit. One hard to break. It's common in the hood to call your mom *moms*. I have no idea why. I tried to leave all the old slang behind. Some things still slip out."

Eve shifted in his lap, feeling his cock stir.

"Like my cock wants to slip out right now." He brushed his fingers up her thigh and under her sundress. "And slip right into you."

Eve look up and down the beach. There was no sign of Cole. Hell, there was no sign of anyone around. "Right here?"

"Yeah. Right here. Right now. Why not?"

She spun around to face him, her legs straddling his. "No condom?"

"No. Unless you're not on the pill."

"I am. But…"

He kissed her, stopping her flow of words. He licked along the inside of her mouth, along her teeth. He licked her bottom lip before sucking on it. "Have you been tested?"

"No, I've had no reason to. I haven't had sex since my husband."

A look crossed his face and she realized that her husband was going to have to be a topic of conversation in the near future. Ren wanted more answers than she had given him so far. And Cole did, too. They had been patient, but...

"I haven't had sex with anyone but you since I've been tested last."

"Except Cole."

His lips thinned. "Yes. But we used a condom. He gets tested regularly though. That I do know."

"Why do you get tested? Are you with that many women?"

"I have been. In the past."

"Don't you use protection?"

"Always."

She remembered reading about the paternity tests he had been ordered to take on a couple occasions. The gossip rags had always admitted his willingness to take them. Most likely because he was confident none of the children would be his. It was probably true that he always used protection. His mom apparently didn't raise a fool, but...

"But now you want to skip it with me?" Her question reflected her surprise. Why now? Why her?

"Yes, I want to fuck you with nothing separating the two of us. I want to feel your heat, your wetness, directly on my skin. If you're not sure about it, I'll go grab a condom. I want you to be comfortable."

She worried at her lip. Her intent was to be long-term with both Cole and Ren. Eventually she supposed they would stop using condoms. And she *was* on the pill, but still...

"Are you planning on fucking anyone but me or Cole?" He asked her.

"No." She turned the tables on him. "Are *you* planning on fucking anyone but me or Cole?"

He laughed and shook his head. Her eyes caught the glint of his diamond earrings. "No, ma'am."

"Good answer. Let me get out of my panties."

"I knew I liked you in that little sundress for a reason besides your shapely legs. And your freckled shoulders."

She gave him a big smile and lifted herself off him enough to pull her panties off one leg; they fell to the ankle of the other one. She kicked them off, but her toe hooked them and Ren ended up wearing them on his head.

They both laughed and he tossed them to the side.

"Now get out your cock. I want to ride it like a bucking bronco."

"Oh, yes ma'am," he said in a bad Midwestern accent. "I'm happy to oblige."

~

By the time Cole appeared at the top of the steps, Ren and Eve were each settled back into separate chairs. The only connection between them was their linked hands suspended between the chairs. Ren took a long pull on his beer as Cole approached them.

Ren's gaze was glued on Cole. She didn't blame him. So was hers.

Cole was shirtless, barefoot, and only wearing tiny running shorts—more like a scrap of fabric. Light and silky, the shorts were plastered to his muscular thighs and the bulge in his crotch. The light sweat made his body shine, the sun catching his curves and planes. His six-pack rippled as he moved toward them.

The urge to lick the salty skin covering his stomach made her pin her thighs together.

"That was a long run," Eve said.

"Yeah, I got a call from Dan a few days ago. He set up a commercial shoot for me next month." He ran his hand down his ripped stomach. "I've got to make these pop."

Eve's eyes followed the trail of his fingers. "You're certainly getting darker in the couple days that we've been here," she said, a little breathless.

"Good genes," he answered, and laughed.

Cole unexpectedly moved behind Ren, wrapping his arms around the other man's chest, leaning down to kiss the back of his neck.

Ren pulled forward, dislodging Cole's arms. "Stop. I'm not your girlfriend. And you're sweaty."

"That is certainly true. You're not my girlfriend. And I am sweaty." He moved over to Eve, drawing her out of her chair and into his arms. Eve certainly didn't pull away from his kiss like Ren. But she did jump from the smack on her ass. A small noise escaped her.

"Wanna fuck?" Cole asked her.

Nothing like getting right to the point. Eve's glance shot to Ren and back quickly.

Cole's brows pinned together. "What." He turned to face Ren. "Did you already fuck? Without me?"

Heat rose into Eve's cheeks. Her lips flattened. Ren looked away. "You did."

Eve tried to pull away. "I need to shower."

"Me, too." Cole tucked a strand of her hair behind her ear. "We can conserve water and shower together."

"No," Ren said, his voice tight.

"Sharing is a part of this, Renny. No jealousy. We can fuck each other separately, or together. We can even fuck each other without Eve. The dynamics are fluid, flexible."

"Won't happen."

Cole made a sound, like he didn't believe it.

"Don't hold your breath," Ren warned him.

Cole shook his head.

"I won't let you fuck me."

"No," Cole answered, suddenly serious. "No, I know you'd top me. I know you won't allow another man to top you, to be the dominant. Right now, I'm okay with that."

Cole stood there a moment longer, waiting for something—

anything—from Ren. When he didn't get a response, he grabbed Eve's hand. "If you scrub my back, I'll scrub yours?"

Eve smiled at the vision his words brought into her head. "That sounds like a plan." She reached her hand out to Ren in invitation. "You coming?"

Ren's nostrils flared. "No."

Cole said, "Your loss!" He gave Ren a big Cheshire cat smile as he dragged Eve behind him. Eve looked back. Ren sat stiffly in his chair, staring at the shoreline.

The steam from the hot shower billowed out into the bedroom. Ren had no doubt they were doing more than taking a shower. The noises coming from the room alone told him that. He leaned against the wall next to the open bathroom door. His fists had clenched without him even being aware of it. He unclenched them, pressing them along his thighs to dry the dampness.

His chest tightened and he closed his eyes, sighing. He wanted to join them. His heart and body were fighting his brain. He was having a hard time swallowing his attraction to another man. Even if it was Cole. His head said it was wrong. His heart said otherwise, encouraging him to walk through the open door. To accept what was freely offered.

Cole was right. No one had to know. Only Cole and Eve, and he trusted them both. He had known Cole long enough that he trusted him with his life. And Eve had done nothing that would make him think he couldn't trust his life in her hands.

His intent when he decided to meet her here at the beach house was for them to spend some time exploring each other. To find out more of the little details about her he was curious about. To find out what made her tick.

He already knew her body well enough—in the past few weeks

he'd explored every inch of it—but he wanted to know her mind, too. She was intelligent, and that made her damn sexy to him. Coupled with her luscious body, she was a home run for him. Or more like a touchdown.

From the get-go, he'd had mixed feelings about sharing her with Cole. He'd never had to share a woman before. If it had been anyone other than Cole…

And he *definitely* had mixed feelings about Cole. He kept tamping down the feelings that wanted to rise to the surface.

But he didn't want to fuck this up. He didn't want to risk Cole's friendship. He didn't want to lose Eve. The thought of losing either of them brought a sharp pain to his chest.

And as much as he wanted to think he had to force his attraction to Cole, he didn't. He just didn't want to admit how much Cole appealed to him. Now that he looked at the man in that light, he wanted Cole as much as he wanted Eve. When Cole had walked practically naked across the deck earlier after his run… Eve was right, Cole was a beautiful man.

Did he want to fight his reaction? Hell yes. His body was playing tug-of-war with itself.

Even now, he was fully erect, listening to the sighs and groans coming from the bathroom. He tried to rile up the anger at his reaction. But he couldn't. *He couldn't.* The anger was not there. He wanted to say it was defeat. But that wasn't true, and to even think that certainly wasn't fair to Cole either.

With determination, he pushed away from the wall and quickly stripped out of his clothes. He stepped into the steamy bathroom.

He stood there for a moment, tying the images to the sounds he heard. They were in a corner of the large glass shower, Eve's cheek and palms pressed against the tiled wall, Cole pressed against her from behind. The breadth of his shoulders and back made it hard for Ren to see her; Cole's body almost completely hid hers. Neither of them had noticed him yet.

An urge shot through Ren. Excitement, want, need. It settled deep inside him, making his cock even harder, his balls even tighter.

He quietly opened the shower door and stepped in, the hot water running in rivulets over his face, down his chest, over his back, down the crack of his ass. He blinked his eyes to clear the water.

He reached out tentatively; his fingers fumbled and faltered over Cole's body, down his back, over the firm curve of his ass.

Cole twisted his head to give him a smile. "About time."

Ren found himself blushing. Actually blushing. He wasn't embarrassed about what was to come, but how he'd been acting, how he'd been resisting.

"I've been an ass."

"But you're here now."

Ren stepped behind Cole to place his mouth where the man's jawline met his neck. Ren wrapped his arms around Cole, his hands searching blindly for Eve's waist. He brushed his fingers down her belly to find her mound. He moved Cole's hand away from her clit, and he took the other man's place. He separated the hot folds, finding her stretched, full from Cole's cock deep inside her. His fingers lingered over Cole's length as the other man slid in and out of her. Ren teased Eve's clit and she cried out in response.

Ren's hard cock was pressed against Cole's tight ass. His gluteal muscles flexed against Ren as the other man tilted his hips, fucking Eve.

He fought the urge to separate those ass cheeks and drive deep into him. But he had no lube and the lube Cole had brought was water-soluble, which would not help either of them.

He spotted the liquid body wash and squirted it into his hands. He slicked his cock up, then slid it between Cole's cheeks. He didn't penetrate, but they nestled his cock perfectly. The soap made their skin slippery enough that with each thrust of Cole's hips, Ren's cock slid between the other man's crease.

Ren sank his teeth into the corded muscle of Cole's shoulder as he rocked against him. His arms tightened around Cole, his hands playing with Eve's clit. Her wet hair covered her face, but her moans were loud and clear. Sounds that drove him crazy. He imagined it was him thrusting deep within her, filling her up, feeling her warm, wet juices all over his cock.

Cole arched his back when Ren bit him harder.

"Oh, fuck, yes," Cole groaned.

Ren soothed the resulting teeth marks with his tongue. He was close. His fingers twitched uncontrollably against Eve's clit. He sank his teeth into Cole's other shoulder. Ren felt himself swell even more before he tensed and shot his load all over Cole's back. The silky ropes of semen were quickly washed away by the cooling water.

Cole shuddered, pumped once, twice, and on the third pump, he cried out.

Eve pushed against Ren's fingers, making her cry out as well. "I'm coming," she called out, and Ren reached up to twist her nipple as he thumbed her clit even harder. She jerked under his fingers, under Cole's limp body.

"She just gushed all over me. I love it," Cole said faintly.

CHAPTER 12

The fire crackled and popped as they sat around it, mesmerized by the flame. The silence between them was peaceful, the crash of the waves a soothing sound outside the circle of firelight.

It was like the three of them were meditating, absorbing each other's calm energy without saying a word. Words weren't necessary, as a feeling of contentment and satisfaction surrounded them all.

An unseen bird squawked as it flew overhead in the dark, breaking the silence.

"I don't want this to end."

Eve hadn't realized she'd said it out loud until the guys both shifted in their seats.

"Won't your friend want to kick us out soon?" Ren asked her. "I don't want to overstay our welcome. It would be nice to be able to use this place again."

"I…" Her voice cracked and Eve cleared her throat. "I have a confession to make."

She was glad the glow of the bonfire hid the redness of her cheeks.

"What?" both men asked at the same time. They glanced at each other before looking back at her. Ren's eyes were narrowed, his gaze searching her face. Cole's face held an easy expression, like there couldn't be anything she could say that would surprise him.

"I should have said something sooner…but I really didn't think it was that important."

"Eve, spit it out before I take you over my lap and spank it out of you," Ren said. Then he laughed. "Damn, that sounds so tempting I may do it anyway."

Eve rolled her eyes at him. "Don't tease if you're not going to follow through."

Cole's slapped his knee. "Oooh, I think that may be a challenge, brother."

Ren's eyebrows rose. "Would you like that?"

Eve bit her bottom lip. She lifted a shoulder. "As long as you don't hurt me." But that could've gone unsaid. Ren wasn't out to hurt her, but rather pleasure her.

Ren rubbed his palms together. "Damn. I can't wait to see your ass pink from me spanking you."

The thought of either of them playfully spanking her, making the skin on her ass red and tingling, sent a thrill down to Eve's toes. Her pussy clenched.

She stood up to approach him.

Ren stopped her with a raise of his hand. "No. Sit down. We want to hear this confession first. Nice try at a distraction though."

With a sigh, she settled back in her seat, facing them over the fire. Where to begin…

"It's really not that big of a deal. I just always want us to be honest with each other."

Cole nodded. "Honesty is good."

Ren gave him a glance. "Honesty is required, as is trust."

Eve knew he wasn't only saying that to her, but to Cole as well. Honesty and trust were a cornerstone of any good relationship, whether it involved two partners or more.

"You can tell us anything." Cole prodded.

"I agree. I…" Both men leaned forward in their chairs as if they were anxious to hear this perceived Holy Grail of secrets. "I actually own this house."

As if synchronized, they both sat back hard, the plastic Adirondack chairs groaning under their weight.

"What?"

"Wait a minute! You don't have a car; you have a tiny little house in the burbs, but this… You own this beach house?" Ren sounded a bit indignant.

"It's my one guilty pleasure…well, besides you two."

Cole winked at her, licked the tip of his index finger before drawing a *1* in the air. "Point for you for that last part."

"Are you a trust fund baby or something?" There was an edge of anger surrounding the question, almost as if Ren bristled at the idea of her coming from money. Especially when he'd had to work so very hard to be successful. Nothing had been handed to him in life.

But she herself was the daughter of a mechanic and a waitress. Her parents had been hard-working folk.

Eve chuckled, trying to lighten his mood. "No, not at all."

"Then how? You've only ever told me that you sit on the board and volunteer at the House to Home Charity. Last time I checked volunteering didn't pay very well. In fact, it pays nothing."

"That's correct," she answered Ren.

"So you're independently wealthy and didn't want us to know?" Ren asked, surprise in his voice.

"No, it wasn't anything like that. I just thought it wasn't necessary to bring up how I can afford a house like this right on the beach."

"Until you were forced to," Ren stated.

"I still didn't have to say anything. I chose to."

"Seriously." Ren's mouth turned down at the corners. Maybe she shouldn't have worded it quite like she did.

"Well, since your spilling the beans, tell us why you still wear a wedding band. Does it have something to do with this house?" Cole asked her.

She watched quietly as Ren got up and threw another piece of driftwood on the fire. It cracked and popped before it settled down.

Ren let out an impatient breath. "Damn, Eve, stop torturing me...*us*. Get to the facts."

"The facts..." She looked up into his face. His expression was hard and appeared a little sinister in the reflection of the flames. "The fact is I was married. My husband was killed."

Cole sank back into his chair. "Damn."

Ren stepped closer to her. "Explain." He squatted beside her, and laid a hand on her thigh.

His touch bolstered her a bit. She laid a hand over his and squeezed his fingers. She always felt better when one or both of them were touching her in some way, connecting with her. And she was about to tell them something she didn't like to talk about. Something she fought hard to not let consume her life.

And though they didn't realize it, this... *This* was why she hadn't told them she owned the house. It was the questions that would follow she just wasn't ready to share the answers to. Not because she didn't trust them, not because she thought it was none of their business. But because every time she talked about it, it was like reopening a festering wound.

"My husband was a doctor—"

"So a doctor, that explains the money," Ren said.

"No," she said softly. "There wasn't money. But there were life insurance policies. I only knew of one. One that each of us had. Apparently, he had a few others I knew nothing about until an estate attorney contacted me." She heard the hitch in her voice. "I guess he worried about me. He worried what would happen if he was killed in one of the countries he worked in when he was overseas with Doctors Without Borders. Some of them are in turmoil and those were always the countries in which he ended up. Where he was needed the most.

"But the funny thing was he survived all of those tours. He'd come back physically and emotionally exhausted, but he always came home.

"One night he was coming home from a shift at the hospital. He was on I-90 when he saw a car pulled over on the berm. There had been an accident. A hit and run apparently, because the striking vehicle was gone. The driver was pregnant and alone. She was bent over in front of her car. Emergency vehicles hadn't gotten there yet. The snow was…"

Ren scooped her out of her chair and sat down with her wrapped in his arms. He kissed her shoulder.

Tears burned her eyes. She hadn't talked about this in so long. She kept it buried deep inside. "He had to help her. He had to. It was his nature. He would not—could not—just drive past someone who needed medical attention.

"He pulled over and was helping her when another car swerved on the slippery road, hitting her car before striking both of them. They were both killed."

She wanted to tell them it wasn't instant, that they both had suffered with fatal injuries until they succumbed to them. That even the baby hadn't survived. But the words wouldn't pass her lips. She closed her eyes. The vision she got in her mind of the scene was once again fresh. Her stomach was an aching knot.

A tear rolled down Eve's face. Ren caught it with his lips.

She whispered, "As bad as this sounds, I wish he hadn't stopped. God, I miss him." She gripped his hands for strength, to keep from sobbing, hiccupping. She didn't want to fall apart in front of them. She had fallen apart one too many times in the months following her husband's death. And eventually when she bought the beach house, she had spread his ashes along the shoreline and into the surf. When she closed the urn that had held his ashes, she had also closed up her grief, ignoring the emptiness inside.

Cole came behind them and wrapped his arms around them. He kissed her hair, murmuring, "I'm sorry."

Eve cupped Cole's jawline and gave him a sad smile.

Ren rubbed her back absently. "Now I understand why you didn't want to talk about it."

She had loved her husband. Still did. But the men wrapped around her now, trying to soothe her sadness, her pain, were starting the fill the place in her heart that had been empty since she'd lost her husband.

She missed the passion, the deep conversations, the silliness, the seriousness of having a significant other in her life. The completeness.

She'd never thought one man could fill her husband's shoes. Never. And maybe in the back of her mind that was the reason she'd thought she needed two. The completeness of Quinn's, Ty's, and Logan's relationship had become a goal for her. She had been envious.

But if she was honest with herself, either of the men holding her could have filled his shoes. Either of them could make her complete. She didn't need both.

But she wanted both. Selfish or not, she now realized she couldn't let either of them go, even after only knowing them for a few weeks, no more than a couple months. She didn't want to live without either of them.

They were hers. She was theirs.

In some cosmic way, they were meant to be together. All three of them.

Was she starting to love them?

Yes, she thought she was.

CHAPTER 13

No one had remembered to shut the curtains last night, so the early morning sun was illuminating the room way too brightly for their tastes. But no one wanted to move to close them.

So now, to avoid the glare in their eyes, they laid on their right sides to avoid the large window, like three spoons nestled in a utensil tray. Cole, Eve, and Ren.

Ren's arm was relaxed and warm as it draped over Eve's ribs. She felt the movement of the muscles barely beneath his ebony skin.

His long fingers trailed back and forth along Cole's hip and up his waist before stopping at the top of his rib cage. It was like absently petting a cat. Soothing. Mindless.

Eve turned her head slightly, and whispered, "You know it's not me you're touching, right?"

A small burst of warm breath tickled the back of her neck. "I know."

"You enjoy touching him, don't you?"

No answer was needed. The proof of his enjoyment was nestled against her buttocks. She wiggled tighter against the heat and the hardness.

Eve placed her left hand over his and intertwined their fingers. As he stroked Cole's skin, so did she.

A deep sigh escaped Cole, causing the lift and fall of his ribs. He was awake. For how long she didn't know, but not one complaint about Ren's touch waking him had escaped his lips. Nor should there be one. Eve knew how happy all this had made him. She wondered if Ren knew just how much.

Cole's back arched enough to press tight against her breasts making her nipples harden. If she turned Cole to face her, she bet her nipples weren't the only things that were hard.

Ren must have had the same thought as his hand slid over Cole's hip, bringing Eve's hand with his.

The two of them, hands still intertwined, discovered that hardness. The heat and silkiness of Cole's skin covering his steely length.

Ren's fingers gripped hers even tighter, controlling her movement, exploring the contrast of Cole's balls to the hardness of his cock. Back and forth from the base of his sac to the top of his cock.

At the top, Eve's thumb caught a drip of precum, and she brushed it around the head before Ren's hand forced her back down to the base. Eve felt Cole's groan before she heard it. The vibration of his body against her caused her nipples to pebble even tighter.

Eve pressed her lips against Cole's neck, giving him a chaste kiss, followed by a dart of her tongue, before sinking her teeth into his skin.

"Fuck."

This long weekend had shown Eve how much she enjoyed being bitten and how much she loved doing the biting. But Cole loved it even more. He couldn't get enough of her or Ren sinking their teeth into his skin. He had said the marks left behind made him feel taken. Possessed. Even owned.

She smiled against the base of his neck, then sucked hard. Pulling away slightly, she could see the small, pink, damp circle she left. She pursed her lips and blew, raising goosebumps on Cole's body.

She nuzzled the crook of his neck as Ren and she stroked him. A rhythm that had a purpose, a goal.

Ren pressed harder against her, shifting enough to slide himself between her legs, his cock wedged between her thighs and pussy. Her toes curled as a line of need rode up her body. It was her turn to groan.

Ren's arm tightened around her waist as his hand tightened around Cole's cock. Eve pushed her buttocks back and up against Ren, making room for him.

With a slow, deep thrust, he filled her wet, throbbing pussy. A gasp escaped her, her breath blowing against Cole's ear.

Ren's hips pick up the rhythm of his hand. For every stroke he made deep within her, his hand mirrored it on Cole's cock. Eve's fingers convulsed around his.

It wasn't a frantic need, but a slow dance. Both men's muscles were tight, bunched, attempting to keep some sort of control.

Eve's eyes fluttered as she concentrated on the stroke of Ren's cock in her pussy, and of his hand on Cole's cock. She wrapped her top leg over Cole's, bringing them even closer.

She could feel the heat building within her, flaring through her body. She was close.

Cole tensed against her with a shuddered breath. He was close.

Ren increased the rhythm among all three of them, stroking faster. His hips, his hand.

With a sharp cry, Cole jerked and released himself. The pulsing under Eve's fingers was all she needed and her pussy closed tighter around Ren's cock as they both came together. Ren muffled a curse against her back, his fingers still twitching on Cole's spent cock.

Muscles relaxed, breathing slowed, but not a word was spoken. They enjoyed the rise and fall of breath with each other. A connection no one wanted to be the first to break.

Eve knew she wanted more of this. More of them.

She snuggled deeper between them. This was where she belonged, she thought, before falling asleep once again.

CHAPTER 14

Ren paced his room. His oversize bedroom now seemed like a cell. He couldn't sleep. He was restless. He wanted to bellow his frustration. His house was too quiet and his bed too empty. This had never been a problem for him before. But now... Now after spending days at the beach house with both Eve and Cole, now he couldn't stand the silence, the thought of everyone going their separate ways. Even if it was only for a night or two.

And never before had he actually felt this lonely.

The idea suggested upon parting, for everyone to go home and take care of business, to get caught up with their responsibilities, sucked. He grunted. Of course, it had been *his* idea.

Dumb ass!

And now this emptiness overwhelmed him, causing a weird pain in his chest.

He tried several times to fall asleep. It was pointless.

Maybe he needed to go downstairs and pour himself a whiskey. Something to take the edge off.

He swallowed hard. He stopped pacing and placed his palms flat against the wall, his head hanging between his arms.

Fuck. Who was he kidding? He didn't need a drink. He needed Eve. He needed Cole.

They did this to him. *They* had made him need them. *They* had sucked him in, making him emotionally dependent.

When had he ever felt this type of attachment to anyone before?

Well, besides his mother, of course.

When did this fucking happen? *How* did this happen?

With an explosive curse, he punched the wall. The drywall crunched under his fist, leaving a hole bigger than his hand. And he didn't care.

He loved them.

He loved Eve. He loved everything about her. Her smile. Her freckles. Her intelligence. Her independence. Her braveness at coming up with a plan to get what she wanted. And then actually making it happen.

How could he feel this way so fast?

He closed his eyes, sucking in a breath. It wasn't just Eve he loved…

He loved Cole. He didn't love him as a brother. He didn't love him as a best friend. Not even like a teammate.

He loved Cole for Cole, for who he was as a person.

Fuck.

He loved him.

His stomach twisted into a knot.

Suddenly, he was very afraid.

Ren flinched at the *ding* of the elevator. At three in the morning, it sounded as loud as a tower bell. The whisper of the air conditioning in Cole's place was the only other noise in the dark penthouse. He kicked off his shoes, so he could walk soundlessly through the condo.

Cole's bedroom door was wide open. When you live by yourself there's no reason to close the door. No privacy needed. Who expects someone to just invite himself over at any crazy hour of the night?

The room was dark. The glow of the digital clock on his nightstand illuminating Cole's face enough that Ren could see he was asleep.

He could still leave. Cole would never know he had been there.

Turn. Leave now. Rethink all of this.

Ren looked at the still figure in the bed. Cole was naked from the waist up, the sheet wrapped around his hips. A bare foot and calf peeked out from the bottom of the tangled bedding.

No. He needed to be honest with himself. He needed to be honest with Cole.

Ren's shaky fingers tore at his clothes. Once he was naked as the man before him, he climbed into bed, careful not to wake him.

Apparently, Cole hadn't had any problems falling asleep. Ren's mouth twisted. No, maybe Ren himself had been the only one feeling the loss tonight.

Big bad "Long-Arm" Landis's heart had finally been sacked.

Cole listened to the soft breathing beside him. Ren's back was pressed against him.

Cole must have kicked the covers off during the night since the temperature of Ren's body was like a furnace. How the hell had he not woken up earlier with this blazing heat next to him?

The sleeping pill he had taken before bed had done its job well. Actually, maybe too well. He hadn't even woken up when Ren joined him in bed. How a man of Ren's size slipped unnoticed into his bed… Cole shook his head. He wouldn't be taking those sleeping pills again anytime soon.

Cole's gaze ran down Ren's exposed body as he slept. Even

though the room was dark, Cole's eyes had adjusted enough to see the dark figure lying next to him.

He reached out to run his fingers over Ren's naked hip. Ren made a sleepy groan and snuggled deeper into the pillow.

He touched Ren's hair. He missed the cornrows, but he couldn't complain too much about his high and tight hair now. Ren was just as handsome with his new style, if not more so.

He wasn't sure why Ren had come over in the middle of the night. But he could guess. Cole had missed Ren, too.

He had voiced his opinion loudly when Ren suggested they all go home for at least a night. Eve had the same feelings as Cole: disappointment. But to compromise, Eve had told Cole she'd see him in a day or two. So, he respected that. He respected the fact Ren needed a little alone time to work a few things out in his head. Eve had even suggested Ren call Ty. Get some advice, some guidance.

The long weekend had been a game changer. Not only for Ren, but for all three of them.

Cole couldn't be happier. Eve couldn't be happier. Now, if only this one would stop stressing...

He ran a finger over the Bulldogs tattoo on Ren's bicep. Brothers for life.

If Cole and Eve had their wish, lovers for life.

Eve had thrown the Hail Mary, now it was up to Cole to get it into the end zone.

And he was good at making touchdowns.

Ren mumbled in his sleep, rolling onto his belly. Cole couldn't resist running his fingertips along the indentation of his spine, the corded muscles surrounding his shoulder blades, the curve in his lower back, the dimples above each ass cheek. And then that ass.

Fuck. That ass.

"Don't even think about it," Ren warned him in a very rough voice.

Cole smile widened. "How can I not think about it? Especially since it's hanging out tempting me."

Cole leaned over to nip at one of Ren's exposed cheeks.

Ren grunted and rolled over onto his side to face him. He ran the back of his hand over his eyes. "Aren't you going to ask me why I'm here?"

"No. I'm just glad you are."

He was so glad he had given Ren the security card for his penthouse after he bought the place, even though he had never, ever thought it would be used for this purpose.

"Did you talk to Ty?"

Ren sat up and shook his head. "No, not yet. I probably know what he's going to say anyway."

"What?"

"That I'm a stupid fuck, that's what."

"Baby—sorry—*Renny*, you're not a stupid fuck."

Ren merely gave him a look.

"Okay, just a little one." Cole leaned close and whispered, "Kiss me."

Ren shook his head. "No."

Cole stared directly into Ren's dark eyes. "Kiss me."

"No."

Cole grabbed Ren's head and pulled him down to kiss him. Ren tensed and he half-heartedly tried to pull away.

Cole kept their lips pressed together, his tongue teasing along Ren's closed mouth. He stroked along his strong, full lips until Ren softened. Just a little. But enough for Cole to take the advantage, to dip his tongue in, to find Ren's. To tease and tangle. His head tilted slightly, enough to seal their lips together fully. Finally... Finally, Ren sighed into Cole's mouth. He closed his eyes and gave Cole what he wanted. Surrender.

Ren grabbed the back of Cole's head with one hand and his neck with the other. He took control, driving their kiss to the edge. Until they had to pull away enough to catch their breath.

Cole smiled. Ren's lips were shiny and a little swollen. Cole went in for a second kiss, but Ren put a hand on his chest to stop him. Well, Cole thought, touching would work, too.

"Dix… Cole, I came over here last night—this morning—for a reason."

"Because you missed touching this sexy, sexy bod?" he teased.

"No. Well, yes. Sort of. But I came here to tell you something."

Cole wasn't going to make this easy for him. "You could've called instead. But after that kiss, I'm not complaining."

Ren shook his head. "No, I had to tell you this in person."

"That you love me?"

Ren's eyes narrowed.

No, Cole was definitely not going to let him off easy. At all. "Of course I know you love me. Brothers for life, man."

"No, it's more than that."

Cole faked a confused expression. "You want to have my baby?"

Ren closed his eyes and took a deep breath. "No, I fucking *love you* love you."

"Oh, like you really *love* me." Cole bit back laughter.

"Yes."

"Well, I love you, too. But you don't want to have my baby?"

Ren hid a smile behind his hands. "You're fucking crazy."

"True. I've been crazy in love with you for years. It's about time you've opened your eyes."

"Whatever, dude. But there's one more thing…"

"The answer is yes! Yes! Yes! Yes!"

"Huh?"

"Yes, I will marry you!" Cole shouted to the ceiling.

Ren frowned. "You're not making this easy on me."

"I know. That's the point, dumb ass. But I already know what you're going to say."

"I want to make sure Eve is a part of our life as well."

"See? I knew it. You love her, too."

"How can I love two people like this at the same time?" Not a question, more like disbelief.

"Easy. But if you need to, do what Eve suggested: talk to Ty. Ask Quinn. Ask Logan. Okay, don't ask Logan, he's not your biggest fan."

Cole fought the urge to order balloons, and cake, and flowers, and champagne. He wanted to celebrate. This was a monumental moment in his life. Almost as big as winning the Super Bowl.

No. It was bigger.

But someone was missing. "What about Eve? We need to tell her."

"Call her. Text her. Right now. Get her over here," Ren insisted. Back to his old bossy self again, Cole was pleased to see.

"It's the ass crack of dawn, Renny. The only cocks crowing right now are ours. I'll text her so when she gets it she can come over. I'll tell the doorman to expect her."

"But tell her to hurry."

Eve rushed into the penthouse, thanking the doorman profusely before the elevator doors glided shut. When she awoke this morning, she found an urgent text message from Cole, asking her to come over as soon as possible. She left so quickly she had even skipped her much-needed coffee. And she didn't do that for just anyone.

As she looked around the penthouse, she froze, listening. But her heart continued to pound wildly, thinking something was wrong. The text had been only a few words. And when she texted back there hadn't been a response.

But now the penthouse was quiet.

Wait. She heard sounds from the bedroom. Cole was in there. She crossed the condo to the master bedroom and the door was ajar.

She tilted her head and listened more carefully. That didn't sound like Cole. That sounded like Ren! And they were certainly not talking.

She pushed the door open.

Cole was on his back on the bed and Ren was over him. They were clearly not struggling or fighting. The only thing wrong with this picture was she was still fully clothed and not on the bed with them! She was going to give Cole a piece of her mind. But later...

Because now...

She walked in to get a better view.

Now, Ren was leaning over Cole. Cole's legs were tucked to his chest and Ren... Ren was fucking him slowly, oh so slowly.

Liquid heat pooled at Eve's center. Her pussy pulsated. What she was seeing turned her on to no end.

Ren was fucking Cole missionary-style. Face to face. He had one hand wrapped around Cole's hard cock, stroking his length as he fucked him.

Eve's knees almost buckled as she watched Ren dance that slow dance, in and out of Cole. There was no anger, but just...tenderness. It was more sensual, and they appeared to have more of a connection. The whole dynamic had changed. This wasn't entirely about sex. Or even just about control or release.

Ren gave Eve a smile before leaning down even further to kiss Cole.

Well, that was new. But it made her happy that he seemed comfortable enough to kiss Cole. What had happened? When?

Honestly, she could care less when that happened, only that it happened.

After Ren brushed his lips over Cole's a couple more times, Cole turned his head toward her and extended a hand. "Are you just going to watch? Or are you going to join us?"

"I don't know. Watching you two is so hot!" But she tore at her clothes, shedding them quickly, kicking her panties off even as she was climbing onto the bed to be with her men.

Her men.

"Come sit on my face."

"Sounds romantic." Eve laughed but certainly didn't turn down the offer. Ren leaned back enough to give Eve room to straddle Cole's head. "Tap out if I start suffocating you."

She lowered her hips and Cole did his magic. Eve sighed as he separated her folds with his fingers and then found her clit with his mouth.

Eve and Ren faced each other. Ren's cock deep in Cole's ass, while Eve moved her hips with Cole's tongue.

Ren leaned in to capture her lips. He kissed her hard and deep, exploring her mouth, one hand still stroking Cole's cock, the other pulling on her nipple. Her nipples drew tighter, and they ached for his mouth.

A brief admiration of how Ren could be that coordinated moved through her. But his fingers, his fist, his cock, his mouth worked her and Cole, until Eve was whimpering and Cole was groaning against her slick cleft. The vibration of the groan against her hypersensitive sex made her jerk and cry out even more.

Ren twisted her other nipple, causing her to grind her hips. Cole banged his hand on the mattress.

"I think he's tapping out," Ren said, a look of amusement passing quickly.

She blinked at Ren's words. Finally, she realized what he'd said. She moved quickly to the side, letting Cole suck in some air.

"Shit. Sorry!"

Cole gave her a crooked smile, his lips shiny and wet. "I'm good at holding my breath, but not that good."

Ren slid out of Cole, both men groaning at the same time.

"But you two didn't come yet."

"Neither did you." Ren told her. "Don't worry, baby. We're all going to come. That's a promise. We're just going to switch it up."

Cole gave Eve a devilish look. "Plus we both came earlier while we waited for you."

"Oh, you did, did you? I see. Now you guys owe me two orgasms."

"Only two?" Ren asked her.

"Well, a few extra wouldn't hurt."

Both men laughed as she smirked at them.

Ren ripped off his condom and handed Cole a fresh one along with the half empty bottle of lube.

Cole nodded and smiled.

What were they conspiring to do?

Ren rolled onto his back and held his hand out to Eve. "Hop on."

She moved until she sank her weight against Ren, enveloping his hard length in between her folds, not letting him penetrate, but only slide between her swollen lips. She rocked back and forth, spreading her wetness over his hard length. When she got to the tip, she paused so he was poised at her entrance. Just right there. *Right there.*

"You're in control," he told her. "You call the plays. *Fuck.* Just don't wait too long."

"What about Cole?" She turned to look at him. He was on his knees behind her, between Ren's legs.

Cole held up the condom and the lube. "Remember when I said I was going to fuck that sweet ass of yours?"

Eve's eyes widened and panic raced through her.

Wait! No. Impossible. She couldn't imagine being stretched that much with them both inside her. Neither of them were small as it was.

Ren took a handful of her ass, flexed his hips, and drove upward. Her tension released with a sigh.

So much for him letting her be in control.

"Sorry, I saw your mind spinning and the panic in your face." Ren gritted his teeth. "It'll be okay, baby, I promise. Don't overthink it."

She really didn't want to think at all. Being on top of him—so deep—she could feel every inch of him.

She gasped as he hit the end of her. He had nowhere else to go.

His fingers dug into the flesh around her hips and he helped lift her up and back down.

Cole wrapped an arm around the front of her shoulders and murmured in her ear, "Don't worry, baby, we'll work up to it."

She heard the words, but it took a moment to comprehend them. Ren's cock impaled her, stretching her already beyond her limits.

She looked down at Ren, her hands braced on his chest. His eyes were hooded, his nostrils flared, his jaw tight. His control was at a breaking point.

"Let's go, Cole… I'm only human, you know," he groaned. He grabbed Eve's hands and pulled them out from under her. She landed on his chest, her breasts pressed tightly against him. Her nipples tightened. His body vibrated like a wire pulled tight, almost ready to snap.

Eve heard the click of the cap on the lube behind her. The cool liquid dripped down her ass crack, pooled around her tight hole, then ran over the heated flesh of her pussy. The cool sensation made her roll her hips.

Ren let out a ragged breath. His eyes squeezed shut, his head rolled back on the pillow.

Eve felt Cole shift behind her, his solid thighs against her ass.

She tensed at the pressure against her slick anus until she realized it was only a finger, smoothing around her rim, teasing her.

The stroke of his finger felt good. It made her want more. Her pussy clenched down, squeezing Ren tight. A wave of pleasure washed over her.

He made a noise like he was going to say something, but he only gritted his teeth and grimaced.

Cole slid his finger into her. After a few movements with the one, he worked a second finger in. She felt stretched and tight, and a little tinge of pain, but Cole kept the rhythm of his fingers in sync with the up-and-down movement of Eve's hips. It was a strange feeling, but… good. Better than she could've imagined.

"How's that, baby?" Cole murmured against her neck. "You feel so tight. So good. I want you to want me inside you. I want you to be begging me."

Eve opened her mouth, but nothing came out. She had no idea she would enjoy Cole's fingers so deep inside her ass.

Eve arched her back slightly as Cole worked his fingers in and out of her.

"Do you want a third?"

Eve pressed her lips together and could only nod.

The pressure increased, the pinch of pain quickly came and went as her body adjusted around him. He was gentle, encouraging.

"Do you want me inside you? Do you want me as deep inside you as Renny is? Do you want us both to make you ours at the same time?"

She did. But another flash of panic shot up her spine. She nodded.

"I couldn't hear you."

She nodded again, struggling to get the words past her lips.

"Is that a yes?"

Fuck. "Yes!" *Fuck yes.*

She felt the broad tip of his cock at her smaller entrance; more lube flowed over and down her. He squirted some liberally on the condom he wore.

"Let her up a little bit," he said to Ren. Ren loosened up on her wrists he'd been holding on to so tightly.

His body stilled underneath her. Waiting for Cole…

Cole wrapped an arm around her belly, supporting her, holding her right where he wanted.

Cole pushed against her, testing her tightness. "Relax," he whispered. "Relax, baby."

Eve closed her eyes and willed herself to relax, to just let go, just let it happen. She was with two people she trusted. Two men who would never intentionally hurt her.

He pressed harder, slowly opening her up to him. When the rim of his head passed the rim of her anus, his long sigh swept over her back. "Oh baby, you don't know how tight you are. How good you feel."

He pushed deeper slowly. Her body, which was still full with Ren, resisted him.

"Oh shit, Cole. I feel you against me," Ren rasped.

"I know. I feel you too. We're now all connected. All one."

Both Ren and Eve cried out as Cole pushed deeper.

Eve thought there was nowhere else for him to go. There couldn't possibly be any more room inside her.

He pulled back a little bit and Ren pushed forward. When Ren pulled back, Cole pushed forward.

Eve felt about to shatter. There was some slight discomfort, but beyond that was the most complete feeling. The fullness, the belonging to both of them at once.

The pleasure built until it radiated from her core, curling her toes, making her eyes roll back in her head.

Her head fell back against Cole's shoulder. Her fingers dug into Ren's chest as she opened her mouth. She released a long, low wail as they took turns thrusting into her.

It was crazy. It was too much. Her body wanted to explode, fall to pieces.

"Holy fuck, she's coming all over me," Ren said, his voice hoarse. "Cole, I can feel both you and her pulsating. I… I can't hold on any more."

"You can. You will," Cole urged him. "I want us to all come together. Eve, tell us when you're going to come."

The alternating thrusts drove her to the edge. But when Cole reached down to stroke her clit with his thumb, she totally came undone.

"Oh God, I'm coming!"

Waves rippled over her, through her, wrapping around Ren's cock as he thrust one more time and released himself deep inside her. Cole jerked against her, jerked again, dropping his forehead to her back, shouting out a curse, then something unintelligible.

A gush of warmness released from her, down her thighs, onto Ren's lower belly as he stilled.

"She soaked me." Ren said it quietly, but the satisfaction was clearly there in his tone.

"I love how wet she gets," Cole said against Eve's skin before sighing.

"You know, I'm in the room here," she reminded them.

"Oh, we know." Ren managed a crooked smile. He appeared too tired to manage anything more.

"You're right where you belong."

CHAPTER 15

E ve had her hand wrapped around her well-needed, well-deserved cup of coffee. The sun was high enough that whatever take-out Cole had ordered would be considered brunch, if not lunch.

They were now collapsed into lounge chairs on the balcony that circled Cole's penthouse. All three of them nursed their coffees, feeling content and tired.

She missed the deck at the beach house, but Cole's place sure did have a beautiful view of the city.

"Soooo…" She had waited long enough to broach the subject she was dying to know about. "I know we didn't get to talk about it, but I'm assuming there was some kind of confession…declaration… something along those lines between the two of you before I got here this morning?"

Ren squirmed in his seat. Cole smiled smugly at her over his coffee mug.

She wanted to yell, *Uh, hello? Can someone just spill the beans?*

But she didn't. Instead she asked them both, "Okay, then… Where do we go from here?"

Cole's expression told her he knew exactly where he wanted

things to go moving forward. Ren's was more shell shocked, as if he hadn't really considered it. He had only thought about the here and now.

He scrubbed a hand over his short hair. Eve watched several emotions cross his face as he gave it some thought.

Eve waited for some epiphany. But in the end Ren simply shrugged. "I have no idea."

"Well, since we all love each other—" Cole announced.

"We do?" Finally! That was why she'd broached the subject in the first place.

"Well, yes. It's clear that—"

Eve interrupted Cole again. "It is?"

Cole blew out a breath and laughed. "Sorry. My bad. *Our* bad. We have something to tell you."

Eve crossed her arms and tilted her head. "Apparently."

With a little smirk, Ren unfolded himself out of his lounge chair and pulled Eve to her feet. He wrapped his arms around her from behind, pulling her to his chest. His deep voice made his chest rumble against her back as he said, "Sorry, I think we missed something important."

Cole broke into a huge open smile as he joined them. He faced the two of them as he stepped close, wrapping his arms around both her and Ren.

Now *this* was a group hug, Eve thought as she sighed, enveloped in their arms. She felt loved and secure and...

Complete.

But she still wanted to hear it.

"Oh, you missed it. Renny declared his undying love for me... How he wanted to marry me and have my baby... That he couldn't live without me... How we're soulmates... And he told me I can call him baby from now on."

"Really," Eve said flatly, keeping her expression blank.

"Yes! It was the most touching thing *ever*."

Eve felt Cole's body shake as he fought the laughter. She tried to twist in their arms to search Ren's face. But they squeezed her tighter between them.

"What Cole meant to say was…we love you."

"Oh."

"Just 'Oh'?" Ren asked, a bit surprised.

"Well, you know. No one wants to have my baby, so I'm feeling a little left out."

Ren groaned. "Can we drop the baby talk?"

Eve chuckled. "Gladly. So, you two love me, huh?"

"We do," Ren answered her.

"And you love each other."

"Yes, and its *love* love," Cole clarified, teasing.

"We do," Ren repeated, ignoring Cole.

"Damn, I love it when a plan comes together."

"Don't get cocky now," Ren warned her.

"Why not? I'm getting two of them now. What a lucky girl I am." She might be playing, but the last part was oh so true. She was really lucky to have not only one awesome man, but two. How many people can say that?

Joy filled her until almost bursting. She had taken a risk, and it had worked out. How about that?

"Well?" Ren asked.

"Well what?" she asked, feigning innocence.

"She's going to make us wait, like we made her wait," Cole scoffed.

A buzzer sounded. The take-out had arrived.

"Saved by the bell," she said.

"No," Ren said. "Don't you dare move, Cole."

"But our food is going to get cold," Eve complained. "And I'm hungry!"

"So you better hurry up," Ren told her.

"Good things take time."

"Eve…" Ren opened his mouth.

"Yes, my love?"

And then shut it.

"Am I your love?" Ren asked, with all the seriousness of a heart attack.

"Oh, absolutely."

"Am I?" Cole asked.

She gave him a wide smile. "You are, too."

"But do you *love* love us?" Cole asked playfully.

Eve laughed. "Yes. I love you both tremendously. You both have captured my heart and filled the empty piece again. And for that I have to thank you." She looked up into Cole's eyes. "I love you, Cole." Cole gave her a quick kiss and let Ren and Eve go. She turned in Ren's arms to face him. "I love you, Ren."

Ren, wearing a huge smile, gave her a quick squeeze and a kiss. He reluctantly released her, too.

"Now, can we eat?" Cole took the words right out of her mouth.

White Chinese food cartons were strewn all over the table. They decided to eat their feast outside since the weather was perfect. And the term *feast* was an understatement. Cole had ordered enough food that they barely put a dent in it before they all fell into a food coma.

Eve pushed her plate away. Ren had served her a generous portion of moo goo gai pan and she managed to polish it all off. She had been starving. But now her belly was full, and she sat back in her chair with a satisfied sigh.

All during lunch the guys talked about upcoming projects their sports agent had set them up with—which got Cole regretting ordering Chinese food since it always got him so bloated and he needed to drop some body fat before his next commercial. You know, make those abs pop and stuff, according to him.

Eve had stayed quiet while listening to the easy rapport between them. It was something natural between the two of them. While at the beach house, she learned they had become fast friends as soon as they met each other on the field, a connection that had easily—okay, Ren might argue how easily—morphed from best friends to lovers.

Lovers. Eve still couldn't believe it. She unobtrusively pinched herself under the table. Yes, this wasn't a dream. It was real.

It was real enough they needed to make some decisions. And if she didn't steer them in that direction, they'd continue to babble on about football and endorsements and workouts, and whatever else men talked about, all the way until dinner.

She cleared her throat to get their attention. "So…like I asked before, where do we go from here? Where are we even going to live? Of course, I am assuming we are moving in together?"

"That would be the next logical step, I guess. So we'll live…" Ren paused in thought for a moment. "In my house."

"My place," Cole said at the same time.

"I hate this penthouse," Ren exclaimed.

"I hate that dark and gloomy house of yours. And who owns a mansion without a pool!"

Ren snorted with disbelief. "I live on a lake!"

"That's not a lake! That's a pond on steroids."

Eve watched the two of them go back and forth like a ping-pong match. Finally, she interrupted. "Well, that settles it; we'll live in my house."

Ren's mouth dropped open before he closed it with a snap. "We can't live in that shoebox of a house. There's no way—"

"No. I meant the beach house. It's large enough for all of us. I can sell my 'shoebox,' as you call it."

"But it's so far from the city. I like being in the thick of things," Cole complained.

"And I like having all the garage space for my car collection."

Eve wanted to hand them both tissues for all the crying they were doing, but threw up her hands instead. "Fine. I'll live in the beach house. You live in your own homes. You can come visit me."

They quickly shut up. The guys looked at each other. Cole scratched his head, and Ren tugged at his earring.

"Well…" Ren started.

She shrugged. "No. I don't want to hear any whining. We *all* live together or none of us lives together."

Cole whistled. "Damn, now we know who'll be wearing the pants in this relationship."

"Take notes, boys, because here is how it's going to be. We will all move out to the beach house. We'll find an empty warehouse or old cannery to rent so you can store all your toys, Ren. We'll keep Cole's place in the city, in case we want to stay overnight for a show, or dinner, or whatever."

"Or if one of us needs a break."

"That too."

"I love that house," Ren said pensively.

Eve gave Ren a look and a raise of her eyebrows. "What do you love more? Cole and me? Or your house."

Ren pretended to think hard about the answer. "I want to be with you two. I realize there's no comparison. It's a house. Living with you two would make a place home. I'll be happy wherever we end up. As long as it's together."

Cole came around and put an arm across Ren's chest and his chin on Ren's shoulder. "Awwww. How sweet. You are the sweetest!"

Ren shook his head and pushed away from him. "Stop."

Eve pinned her lips together, fighting back the laugh so wanting to escape. "Cole may be trying to get under your skin, Ren, but he's right. That was really sweet."

Cole snapped his fingers and perked up. "We need to declare our love to the whole city."

"Like a press release?" Ren frowned.

"No. Now. Right now. Shout it to the whole world. Come here to the railing."

Eve lifted a brow at him. She wasn't a fan of heights. And getting close to the railing of a balcony that was umpteen floors up was not on her to-do list any time soon.

"Have you lost your mind? No one will hear it." Ren shook his head.

"We'll hear it. Well, and the pigeons. And maybe some neighbors below me." Cole held out his hand to Eve.

She froze. Her gaze bounced between his hand and the edge of the railing.

Ren came over and rubbed her back. "Cole, she just turned white and is now green. I think we'll have to pass on this announcement of yours."

Cole shrugged and turned to face the city. He slapped his right hand over his heart, threw his left arm toward the sky, and tilted his head back.

Eve didn't know if he was going to belt out a song or quote Shakespeare.

He crowed, "The world is my oyster, and I'm too hungry to eat just one."

Ren laughed and shook his head. "Damn, Dix, but that was just… wrong on so many levels."

When Cole stepped away from the railing to help to clear the table, Eve let out a relieved breath.

"I think we're the oysters," Eve said to Ren. She gathered empty containers and patted Cole on the shoulder as she walked by him into the house. "Stick to football. Sadly, you'll never be a thespian."

Cole rushed after her. "Hey, I can act! I've been in plenty of commercials."

Ren followed him in, his hands full of plates and silverware. "You were only there to be the beefcake."

"One day I might be in a reality show just like you were."

Ren looked at him seriously. "I wouldn't wish that on anyone. It was miserable."

Eve couldn't wait to hear *that* story.

EPILOGUE

E ve rolled over with a groan and hit something solid. She opened one eye. Cole. On the other side of her Ren stirred at hearing his "We are the Champions" ringtone start once again. He let out a curse, searching the nightstand for his cell phone. A lamp teetered dangerously as he felt around the table's surface.

He barked out a grumpy "What?" into the phone.

Then he was quiet. After a few moments, Eve rolled toward him to watch his expression as he listened to the person on the other end.

He was not pleased at whatever the caller was telling him.

Finally, he said, "Fuck. Yeah. Okay. I'll call you back."

Eve sat up. "Everything okay?"

Ren released a long breath. "Shit. Someone grab a laptop." Ren reached out his hand impatiently. "Or a tablet. Something!"

Eve elbowed Cole, who grunted and turned his head with a sleepy yawn. "What…"

"Hand me your iPad," Eve said.

Cole gave her a little smirk. "It's right there. Come crawl over me and get it."

"Now's not the time, Cole. Hand me your iPad," Ren said, a little more demanding than Eve.

Cole pushed himself up with a perplexed frown. "Did I miss something?" He snagged his tablet and handed it across Eve to Ren.

Eve watched Ren swipe and press and tap on the screen until he found what he was looking for. He cursed.

He turned the iPad to show them.

Pictures of her and Cole, and her and Ren, were plastered all over the screen with the headline: IS THIS MYSTERIOUS WOMAN STEPPING OUT ON ONE OF THESE SUPER BOWL CHAMPS, OR BOTH?

Before she could even read the first line of the article he pulled up another one: IS "LONG-ARM" LANDIS BEING TWO-TIMED BY HIS GIRLFRIEND?

Then another one: NO RESPONSE FROM COLE DIXON ABOUT THE WOMAN SEEN ON HIS ARM. Had Cole even been asked? Probably not, or he would have said something.

And another: DID COLE DIXON STEAL HIS BEST FRIEND'S GIRL?

All of them included pictures of them as couples, but never the three of them together.

Eve groaned inside. Now that things were falling into place between the three of them, was this media hoopla going to screw it all up?

Cole shrugged a shoulder. "Those pictures were from weeks ago."

"No, look, not all of them." Eve pointed one out to Ren. "That one was from the other day. You and I meeting with the real estate agent." She stared at the photo of her and Ren coming out of a café. They had met with the agent to discuss her listing both of their homes. They were holding hands and smiling at each other.

Eve leaned closer to examine another photo. It was of her and Cole kissing, Cole's arms wrapped around her. She couldn't even remember where it could've been taken. She groaned, running a hand over her face.

Cole grabbed the iPad from Ren and swiped through some of the pictures. "Hey, that's a good one of me!"

"Jesus, Dix." Ren tore the tablet back out of his hands and turned it off.

"Well, we could deny the rumors or simply admit them publicly. Pull the wind out from these paparazzi's sails," Cole said, now more seriously.

"That simple, eh?" Ren asked, his lips pressed into a tight line.

"Yeah, why not?" Cole questioned.

"I agree with Cole. I don't want to be looking over my shoulder all the time for photographers in the bushes. And I certainly don't want people thinking either of you are being played by the same woman. Which, by the way, just happens to be me." Eve frowned.

"Well, are we going to face this head-on? Or are we going our separate ways to avoid this whole thing?" Cole asked, knowing full well Ren wouldn't pick the second choice, but trying to encourage Ren to get on board with him and Eve and be open about their relationship.

"Hell no," Ren said fiercely. Eve relaxed a little bit at his answer.

"Right. So we need to deal with this one way or the other," Cole said.

"Once again, Cole is right." Eve agreed. "We need to approach this on our terms."

Cole gave her a look. "What do you mean 'once again'? I'm right a lot."

Eve rolled her eyes and patted his thigh over the tangled sheet. "I know you are, baby."

"Well, whatever we decide, all three of us have to be on board," Ren said.

Eve once again agreed. "But I'll go along with whatever you two decide. The only reason these people are even interested is because you two are famous. I'm a nobody."

Ren played with a long strand of her hair. "You're not a nobody. Don't say that." He leaned over to kiss her temple.

"You know what I meant."

Cole chimed in. "I'm all for going public. Get them off our back."

Ren was quiet as he stared at the powered-down tablet in his lap. "I'll call Dan back. I'll have him set up a press meeting."

"A press meeting? Really?" A feeling of dread came over Eve. "Do you really think that's necessary? Won't they just get bored after a while, until a new story comes along?" She couldn't imagine standing in front of a bunch of gossip rag writers and whoever else shows up to those types of things to explain to the world about their relationship.

When Cole mentioned going public, she'd thought that meant maybe a press release or having their agent send out a statement. That sounded a little more reasonable.

Eve had never wanted to be in the public spotlight.

I guess I should've thought of that before I tried to hook up with two pro football players. Out loud she said, "Are you sure you want to do this? Don't you think this may get the spotlight targeted on us even more?"

Cole gave her a slight squeeze. "Welcome to our world. This is one of the unfortunate consequences of being a part of it. It'll be okay. I promise."

"I'll call Dan and run this by him. This is nothing new to him since he's also Ty's agent." Ren gave Eve a reassuring smile. "We'll see what he has to say and go from there."

Within two days they stood in the lobby of their agent's office building. Dan was already outside at the entrance to the building, in front of a podium full of microphones.

Eve was amazed at how many sports television stations, newspapers, and magazines were interested in this story. It always surprised Eve how interested people were in other people's lives. She understood it was part of the life of being a public figure, whether a politician, an actor, or a sports star.

Her husband had always been humble about being a doctor, preferring to help people rather than worrying about being rich or in the spotlight.

Dan peeked his head in the door, "C'mon. They're ready for you,"

Eve took a shaky breath.

"I'll take the lead and field the questions," Ren said.

Of course, he would. He wanted to be in control of this interview. His plan was to keep it "short and to the point," as he had said.

"Ready?" Ren asked them.

The three of them gave each other reassuring smiles, as well as "I love yous". They linked arm in arm, Eve in the middle, flanked by her two adoring men. They were about to tell the whole world they loved each other…

They pushed the double doors open and stepped out to a barrage of camera flashes.

Sign up for Jeanne's newsletter to learn about her upcoming releases, sales and more! http://www.jeannestjames.com/ newslettersignup

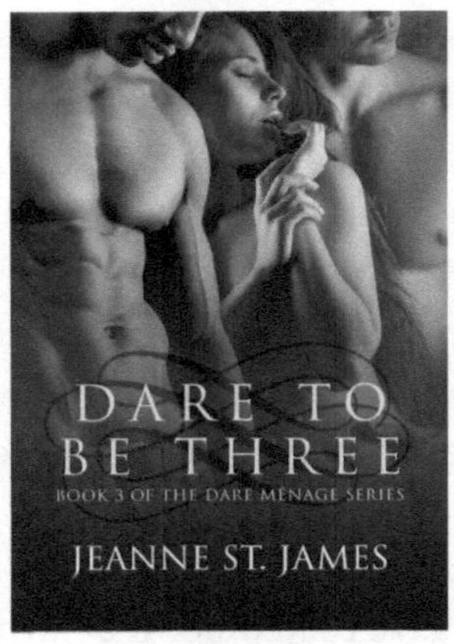

As soon as she spots him, she can't keep her eyes off him…

When Paige Reed spots a man across the room at a party, she's fascinated and decides she wants him in her bed. Fortunately, her husband, Connor, doesn't mind. He's attracted to the powerful man too.

Always bi-curious, the right opportunity has never presented itself to Connor Morgan. Until now. He doesn't mind bringing another man into their marriage as long as it doesn't drive a wedge between him and Paige.

Former NFL player, Graedon Ward likes to be in control. He's more than pleased with Paige's obvious interest. However, she makes it quite clear: it's a package deal. If he wants her, he has to take on her husband too, and past experience has taught him that's a dangerous road to travel.

The chemistry between the three is explosive, but it's Grae's desire to share the same level of intimacy he sees between Paige and Conner that puts real pressure on the threesome. And it may cause it all to crash and burn.

Turn the page to read the first chapter of the third book in The Dare Menage Series: Dare to be Three

DARE TO BE THREE - CHAPTER ONE

He was dark. So dark, the rich, deep tone of his skin reminded her of a ripe plum. She couldn't ever remember seeing someone quite so black. Because of this, her gaze kept drawing back to him. It was rude to stare, she knew, but she didn't seem to have any control over it. She couldn't keep her eyes off of him.

His head looked smooth and beautifully shaped. He had the type of structure which made bald look good.

Never a fan of facial hair, Paige Reed rarely liked it on a man. But this man's goatee was neatly trimmed and fit his face perfectly. A thick gold hoop earring hung from his left ear. He wore a well-tailored suit. He probably had no choice but to get his suits either made for him or, at the very least, tailored to fit. His shoulders were broad, his thighs thick.

She thought her brother-in-law was built like a beast, but this man outsized him. He was enough to intimidate anyone crossing his path.

But not Paige.

He fascinated her.

"You find him attractive, don't you," her husband's whisper came, close to her ear.

Not posed as a question, but she answered anyway, "Yes."

"I'm not sure why you married me, then. I'm as pale as a person can get," he teased.

Paige brushed her fingers through Connor's dirty blond hair, ruffling it a bit. "No, you're not. You worship the sun. And it was that sexy Aussie accent of yours that caught my attention."

"It made you wet."

Paige half-shrugged and gave him a smile. "Still does."

Connor brushed away a strand of hair from her cheek. "Hmm. Good to know. But you like him."

"He's *interesting.*"

"He's dark," Connor stated.

"Yes."

"His skin tone is extraordinary. I like it too."

"Should I be jealous?" she asked.

"Should I?" Connor's vibrant blue eyes twinkled.

Paige laughed, shaking her head. "We've talked about this. Jealousy is not allowed."

"I wonder what he'd say if he knew what we were talking about."

"Or thinking," she added.

"He'd probably run like hell."

"I don't know. I'd hope not." Paige regarded the man across the room talking to her brother. "I've never seen him before. I wonder how well the guys know him?"

"Could be Quinn's friend. Or a former co-worker of hers," Connor suggested.

"Coming to Ty's fortieth birthday party? I doubt it."

"Maybe he's related to Ty."

"*Maybe* we need to stop speculating and ask," Paige suggested.

"You want him." Again, not a question. Just more of an, *are you sure?*

"Do you?" she asked.

"I like what I see. But I need to find out what's up here." He tapped his temple.

Suddenly, Tyson White slipped between the two of them and squatted. Even though the man had retired from the NFL years ago, he was still in extremely good shape, and his shoulders were wide enough to brush against them both.

Not that Paige was going to complain. She and Connor always flirted with Logan's boyfriend, now husband. But it was always in good fun. Ty loved it and neither Logan or Quinn, their wife and mother of their child, minded.

Ty cocked his eyebrow at Paige. "Why are you staring at Grae like a piece of meat?"

"Was it that noticeable?" she asked, surprised.

"Uh, yeah. Hard to miss."

Paige shrugged. "He's hot." *Grae.* What an interesting first name. She wondered what it was short for. Maybe it was a nickname.

Ty looked behind him for a second at the subject in question, then turned back to Paige. "Yes, he is."

"Who is he?" she asked. "Current or former player?"

"Retired. Sort of. Left the NFL after a debilitating medical issue."

"Like what?"

"Like, I'm not telling you his secrets. You'll have to find out for yourself. And anyway, why are you guys so interested?" Ty asked, suspicion thick in his question.

Hmm. The man was a mystery she might have to solve.

Connor spoke up, "Well, you know, there's a certain man I've been trying to get into my bed for a couple years now, but for some reason, he keeps resisting."

Ty lifted his left hand and pointed to his ring finger. "I'm married if you've forgotten."

Connor chuckled. "I haven't."

"And I have a kid." His face lit up. "And another on the way."

"Oh, shit. Congratulations! You sure Quinn wants everyone to know?" Paige asked him.

"You aren't everyone. You're family. But keep it on the D.L. since it's early yet." Her brother-in-law pushed himself to his feet and stepped back from the table. "C'mon. I'll introduce you to Graedon. I won't warn him about the depraved things you two are probably planning for him."

"Oh *please*," Paige retorted as she stood and took Ty's arm on one side, her husband's on the other.

Ty escorted them over to Paige's brother, Logan, who had been deep in conversation with this mystery man.

"Hey, hot stuff," Ty greeted his husband. "Should I be jealous that you've been talking to this handsome hunk of a man for an hour now?"

Logan offered his hand, and Ty took it. Logan drew the darker man into his side, his arm slipping around his waist.

Darker, Paige thought, but not nearly as dark as this...*Graedon*. She liked the name on her tongue.

And that wasn't the only thing she'd like on her tongue.

Wow. She shook her head. She normally wasn't this depraved. Something about this man just drew her in like a fly to honey. Paige held out her hand. "Hi. I'm Logan's sister, Paige."

Graedon gave her a slight smile and, with a quick flick of his eyes, looked her up and down—didn't *that* make goosebumps flood her body—before clasping her offered hand within his.

His grip felt warm and firm, and his hand dwarfed hers. Paige marveled at the contrast of their skin. Their clasped hands reminded her of a yin and yang symbol: opposites, but complementary.

Connor cleared his throat.

Paige released the man's hand, heat climbing into her face, though it seemed Graedon was in no rush to break the contact either.

Logan waved a hand towards Connor. "Grae, this is my brother-in-law, Connor Morgan. The poor sap stuck with Shorty."

Paige glared at her older brother. He knew she hated that nickname.

"Shorty." The name rolled smoothly off Graedon's tongue, and he seemed reluctant to pull his attention away from her to shake Connor's hand. The men's handshake was quick and firm. "Graedon Ward," he introduced himself to Connor.

"Interesting first name," Connor told him.

"Interesting accent," Graedon remarked.

"Connor is Australian," Ty explained.

"And Shorty's husband," Connor said, jerking a thumb towards Paige.

Paige whacked him in the arm. "You know I hate that nickname!"

"Well, I can't tell him my other pet names for you." Connor smiled at Graedon and wiggled his eyebrows.

"He's got a thing for brothers," Ty warned Graedon.

Graedon looked over at Connor in surprise. "Oh?"

"He's not the only one," Ty added, tilting his head toward Paige.

"I'm sorry. I didn't mean to stare so rudely," Paige said, grimacing at Ty's comment.

"Okay then! On that note, we need to go mingle, old man," Logan said as he drew the birthday boy away.

"You're older than me," Ty griped.

"But I look younger," Logan said, as they moved away.

Paige's gaze bounced back to Graedon. "So…"

"You don't mind your wife staring at other men?" It was a serious question but touched with a sense of amusement.

"Well…" Connor pursed his lips for a second. "It depends."

"On what?" Graedon asked, once again clearly surprised.

"On who she's staring at."

Graedon shook his head, obviously confused. "You're not worried she might be interested in the man she's staring at?"

"Oh, I definitely know she's interested in who she's staring at."

Paige waved her hand between the two of them. "Hello! I'm standing right here. Jeez."

"I'm truly sorry, Paige," Graedon said, bowing his head to her. "That was rude of us."

She blinked. Rude? Not unlike her staring.

Now, since she stood next to him, she realized how large a man he truly was. Though she *was* small, or nicely put, petite, hence the "Shorty" nickname. She had to look from her five-foot-two inches up to Connor's six-foot-one. But this Graedon, he had to be an inch or two taller than her husband. While Connor wasn't skinny, the other man definitely outweighed him by—Paige guessed—at least fifty pounds. His hands were large, his fingers long. Good for gripping a football, of course. She wondered how old he was and how long ago he left the game. "How do you know Ty?"

"We played football together in college."

"Ah. And you went on to be pro?"

"Yes, I was lucky enough to be drafted."

"You retired?"

Graedon hesitated for a few seconds, then answered, "Yes, a while ago."

All right, she didn't want to keep bombarding him with questions. She definitely wanted to get to know him better, but she didn't want it to seem like an inquisition.

Oh, but she had so many questions on the tip of her tongue.

What do you do for a living now? How old are you? Do you live around here? Would you like to have sex with my husband and me?

The last one might be a little much. She certainly didn't want to scare him away. And here she thought she would be bored at Ty's fortieth birthday party, but then she spotted his man. She realized she was staring again and her face became heated. "I need to get a drink. Anyone else?"

"I'll get it, honey," Connor said, placing a hand on her shoulder. "What do you want?"

"Something with alcohol. Surprise me." Connor knew her tastes well, so she wasn't worried he'd come back with a drink she didn't like. *Wait.* Had she ever met a drink she didn't like? *Oh, yeah. Gin and tonic. Blech.*

"Anything for you Graedon?"

"A gin and tonic, please. Thank you." He gave Connor a wide smile.

Paige swore it just lit up the whole room. Of course, he would want a drink she hated. But she wouldn't judge him for it. Much, anyway.

"I'll be back shortly," her husband said, kissing her cheek then heading toward the makeshift bar in the corner of the large room.

Her eyes never left Graedon while her husband kissed her—while his, in turn, never left hers. Until her nipples beaded under the thin fabric of her dress—then his gaze dropped but quickly returned to her face.

"I don't know how you can drink that awful shit."

"It's an acquired taste." He studied her face.

Paige tried not to squirm as he ran his gaze from the top of her head to her chin, then just high enough to land on her lips. She unconsciously licked them and then tugged on her bottom lip with her teeth. "I don't think any drink that you need to learn to appreciate is worth drinking. So many other choices."

He stared at her mouth while she talked. She fought the urge to dig into her clutch purse to reapply her lip gloss.

"Choices are wonderful, but sometimes you want one specific thing. So, you work for it until you achieve it."

"We're still talking about drinks, right?" she asked.

He finally raised his eyes to meet hers as a wince of surprise and then clarity flickered in his gaze. Like he'd shaken himself mentally, getting out of some sort of fog.

She hoped it meant that he felt attracted to her.

Suddenly, he leaned toward her, and she froze. He reached out and whisked away something on her face with his thumb.

She stared at him curiously.

He held his thumb up. "Eyelash. Make a wish."

Paige knew exactly what she would wish for. She pursed her lips and blew lightly, the eyelash spinning towards the floor.

"I hope your wish comes true," he murmured, not breaking their locked gaze.

"Me too." Little did he know *he* was her wish.

The seconds ticked by and neither even blinked.

His eyes were like very deep wells of dark brown. Dangerous if you fell in. His thick eyelashes were surely the envy of some women. His lips were dark and thick, reddish at the center like he'd been sucking on a cherry. Those luscious lips parted...

Paige waited for the words to escape, to flow over her. She just knew he was about to say something intriguing.

"Sorry, there was a line at the bar." Connor approached, handing her a tall glass filled with pinkish-red liquid, a maraschino cherry, and a tiny plastic straw. He handed Graedon a short glass filled with ice, a lime wedge, a stirrer, and the clear toxic mix that made Paige scrunch up her nose.

Graedon nodded at Connor, thanking him.

He was such a gentleman, but one she bet knew how to be not-so-gentle at the right times. She covered her sigh by sipping on her drink. She had no idea what the concoction was, but it tasted fruity, and it went down smooth.

Connor upended a beer bottle and took a swig. Some local microbrewery. No piss water—what Paige called regular beer —for him.

"So, what do you do for a living, Connor?" Graedon asked after squeezing his lime wedge and stirring his drink.

Connor slid his arm around Paige's waist and gave her a small squeeze.

Graedon's eyes followed the gesture and didn't raise until Connor answered.

"I'm a structural engineer."

Graedon contemplated the answer. "Structural. Like bridges?"

Connor shrugged slightly. "Yes, bridges. But I mainly concentrate on sports complexes. Like stadiums, arenas, and what not. Anything sports related."

Graedon raised his eyebrows. "Football stadiums?"

Connor nodded. "Yes, some."

"Sounds like a very interesting career."

"It is. But I have to travel a lot."

"Is that how you met your stunning wife?"

Stunning. *Huh*. Paige never considered herself stunning. This had always been a description for leggy blondes who strutted down runways. Cute, maybe. She was short, with long brown hair. Then add some freckles, which didn't make sense for her complexion. Her whole family had been confused about this. Mailman's daughter, Logan had always teased her, which had always upset their single mother.

But it did make her wonder. Especially, since Logan was a foot taller than her and didn't have a single freckle.

Connor gave her a look before answering him, "Yes. We actually did meet at a football stadium. She was with her brother when he was there to re-sod the field."

Paige remembered that day. Logan's business was just getting off the ground and, since she'd been helping him with the business's books, he had asked her to go along because he didn't have any employees at the time. It had been long days laying sod, and they were both filthy and exhausted come nightfall. She felt glad she no longer helped with the physical part of the business.

Then, she reminded herself, if she hadn't gone, she never would have met the crazy, sexy Aussie, who currently had her pinned to his side. The rest was history. Connor picked up his life and moved to the states, gladly making her hometown his, and they got married a few years ago.

Now, with Quinn doing the books and Ty as Logan's partner, the business was extremely successful, and Paige did whatever the guys needed her to do, either on the sod farm, in the office, or out on a job. A sort of Girl Friday/project manager with a great salary and benefits. If they needed coffee, she got coffee. If they needed her on site at a sodding job supervising employees, she was there. The job was never boring. The guys and Quinn relied on her. Sometimes to simply babysit their son Preston.

"Best day of my life," Connor stated, giving her another squeeze.

"Yes, you're certainly a lucky man," Graedon said slowly, the words rolling off his tongue like molasses.

"You could be too."

Paige elbowed her husband. *Too soon.*

Graedon tilted his head and studied Connor. "What do you mean?"

"I just meant one day you'll meet the girl of your dreams." Connor tripped over his words as he added, "That's if you're not already married. I shouldn't assume."

"I prefer women over girls. And, no, I'm not married."

Paige's gaze flicked to his left hand. The only ring this man wore was the one in his ear.

"Yes, a woman," Connor murmured. "One that knows what she wants, when she wants it, and how to get it." He shifted his left arm up to her shoulders.

Once again, Graedon followed his movement until he pinned his gaze to Paige's lips once more. "And you, Paige?"

And me what? Oh. "I help out with Logan and Ty's business."

"I'm sure that keeps you busy. Their business is extremely successful."

"It is. Who expected growing grass could be so lucrative?"

He cracked a slight smile. "I'll have to come out and tour the farm one of these days."

Paige tamped down the urge to rub her palms together in anticipation. *'Will you walk into my parlor?' said the Spider to the Fly.* "Yes, please do. Just let me know, and I can personally escort you."

Graedon tipped his head graciously.

"She's crazy behind the wheel of the UTV. So, I'm warning you now…"

Graedon looked confused. "UTV?"

"Utility Task Vehicle. Like an ATV for farm use," Paige explained.

"However, don't listen to him. I have a safe driving record." *The way into my parlor is up a winding stair.'* "You'll be perfectly fine in my hands." *'And I've a many curious things to show when you are there.'*

"I'm sure I will be," Graedon murmured.

'Oh no, no,' said the little Fly, 'To ask me is in vain, for who goes up your winding stair-can ne'er come down again.' "Why don't I give you my number, and you can text me when you want to come out."

His smile appeared and then disappeared as quickly as it came. A blink and it would've been missed. "Only if your husband doesn't mind."

"Connor doesn't mind, do you, honey?" she asked her husband, without even so much as peek his way.

"No, not at all."

Graedon dug out his cell from an inner pocket of his suit jacket. A few seconds later, he was ready. Paige didn't hesitate to spill her digits.

"Morgan?"

She shook her head. "Reed. I didn't change my name."

Once again, he cocked a brow. Paige thought this might be a signature expression for him.

He slipped his cell back inside his jacket and pulled out a business card. "So you know it's me calling."

Paige tried to pluck it from his fingers, but he resisted just enough so her hand had to make contact with his. The brush of their fingers made her suck in a breath and warmth radiate from her core.

Damn. If this was her reaction to just a light touch, she couldn't imagine how she would respond to something more substantial. But she didn't want to imagine; she wanted to *know*. She let her hand drop, the card ignored in her grasp.

Connor placed his left hand at the small of her back and extended his right hand out to Graedon. "Excuse us, we need to go visit with Quinn. I don't want her to think we're ignoring her tonight."

The larger man shook Connor's hand, then turned to Paige. He dipped his head. "It was nice meeting you tonight. I look forward to the tour."

"It was nice—" *staring at* "—meeting you also. Hopefully, it'll be soon."

Then with that, Connor steered Paige out of earshot. "What do you think?" Connor asked her, barely-contained excitement in his voice. "He's intelligent, well-spoken, hot as fuck."

"Oh, he's a big fat yes. But I wasn't getting any vibes from him other then he's a het."

"Yeah, he was hard to read except when it came to you. He was definitely drawn to you. I think I should be jealous."

Paige bumped her shoulder into him as they walked. "Stop. If you need to make the rules, then make them. If I meet up with him and you don't ever want me to have sex with him without you, then I'll agree to that. I don't ever want you to feel left out, honey."

"We'll discuss it. We'd have to find out if he has any proclivities toward men. If not, that shoots the plan all to hell."

"Plan? Now we have a plan?"

"You had a plan the first second you laid eyes on him across the room, whether you knew it or not."

Paige pursed her lips in thought. "Yes, you're right. As soon as I saw him, I knew I wanted him."

"See?"

"But I want to try to get to know him better if he comes out to the farm. And I have this." She lifted the business card so she could read it. "You could always ask him out for a business lunch or coffee."

"I would need a good excuse other than, 'my wife and I want you to join us in bed.'"

Paige snorted. "You never know, maybe he likes direct."

"Yeah, like he wants to take you directly to bed. He's definitely fascinated by you as well."

"Well, that's a good start."

Connor pushed his way through French doors which opened to a dark patio. Outside, the breeze felt cool, and Paige shivered.

Connor removed his suit jacket and wrapped her in it, pulling her into his arms. "So, what does his card say?"

She held the crumpled card up. "Too dark to read it."

Connor lifted a hold-on-a-second finger and dug his cell phone out. With a push of a button, the card was illuminated.

Paige tried to smooth it out a bit and peered closer. "Graedon C. Ward, College Scouting Director, Boston Bulldogs."

Get *Dare to be Three* here:
www.books2read.com/Dare2B3

IF YOU ENJOYED THIS BOOK

Thank you for reading Daring Proposal. If you enjoyed this story, please consider leaving a review at your favorite book retailer and/or Goodreads to let other readers know. Reviews are always appreciated and just a few words can help an independent author like me tremendously!

Find my complete reading order here:

https://www.jeannestjames.com/reading-order

* Available in Audiobook

Standalone Books:

Made Maleen: A Modern Twist on a Fairy Tale *

Damaged *

Rip Cord: The Complete Trilogy *

Everything About You (A Second Chance Gay Romance) *

Reigniting Chase (An M/M Standalone) *

Brothers in Blue Series:

Brothers in Blue: Max *

Brothers in Blue: Marc *

Brothers in Blue: Matt *

Teddy: A Brothers in Blue Novelette *

Brothers in Blue: A Bryson Family Christmas *

The Dare Ménage Series:

Double Dare *

Daring Proposal *

Dare to Be Three *

A Daring Desire *

Dare to Surrender *

A Daring Journey *

<u>**The Obsessed Novellas:**</u>

<u>Forever Him</u> *

<u>Only Him</u> *

<u>Needing Him</u> *

<u>Loving Her</u> *

<u>Tempting Him</u> *

<u>**Down & Dirty: Dirty Angels MC Series®:**</u>

<u>Down & Dirty: Zak</u> *

<u>Down & Dirty: Jag</u> *

<u>Down & Dirty: Hawk</u> *

<u>Down & Dirty: Diesel</u> *

<u>Down & Dirty: Axel</u> *

<u>Down & Dirty: Slade</u> *

<u>Down & Dirty: Dawg</u> *

<u>Down & Dirty: Dex</u> *

<u>Down & Dirty: Linc</u> *

<u>Down & Dirty: Crow</u> *

<u>Crossing the Line (A DAMC/Blue Avengers MC Crossover)</u> *

<u>Magnum: A Dark Knights MC/Dirty Angels MC Crossover</u> *

<u>Crash: A Dirty Angels MC/Blood Fury MC Crossover</u> *

<u>**In the Shadows Security Series:**</u>

<u>Guts & Glory: Mercy</u> *

<u>Guts & Glory: Ryder</u> *

<u>Guts & Glory: Hunter</u> *

<u>Guts & Glory: Walker</u> *

<u>Guts & Glory: Steel</u> *

<u>Guts & Glory: Brick</u> *

<u>**Blood & Bones: Blood Fury MC®:**</u>

<u>Blood & Bones: Trip *</u>

<u>Blood & Bones: Sig *</u>

<u>Blood & Bones: Judge *</u>

Blood & Bones: Deacon *

Blood & Bones: Cage *

Blood & Bones: Shade *

Blood & Bones: Rook *

Blood & Bones: Rev *

Blood & Bones: Ozzy

Blood & Bones: Dodge

Blood & Bones: Whip

Blood & Bones: Easy

Beyond the Badge: Blue Avengers MC™:

Beyond the Badge: Fletch

Beyond the Badge: Finn

Beyond the Badge: Decker

Beyond the Badge: Rez

Beyond the Badge: Crew

Beyond the Badge: Nox

<u>**COMING SOON!**</u>

Double D Ranch (An MMF Ménage Series)

Dirty Angels MC®: The Next Generation

WRITING AS J.J. MASTERS

The Royal Alpha Series:

(A gay mpreg shifter series)

The Selkie Prince's Fated Mate *

The Selkie Prince & His Omega Guard *

The Selkie Prince's Unexpected Omega *

The Selkie Prince's Forbidden Mate *

The Selkie Prince's Secret Baby *

ABOUT THE AUTHOR

JEANNE ST. JAMES is a USA Today bestselling romance author who loves an alpha male (or two). She was only thirteen when she started writing and her first paid published piece was an erotic story in Playgirl magazine. Her first romance novel, Banged Up, was published in 2009. She is happily owned by farting French bulldogs. She writes M/F, M/M, and M/M/F ménages.

Want to read a sample of her work? Download a sampler book here: BookHip.com/MTQQKK

To keep up with her busy release schedule check her website at www.jeannestjames.com or sign up for her newsletter: http://www.jeannestjames.com/newslettersignup

www.jeannestjames.com
jeanne@jeannestjames.com

Newsletter: http://www.jeannestjames.com/newslettersignup
Jeanne's Down & Dirty Book Crew: https://www.facebook.com/groups/JeannesReviewCrew/
TikTok: https://www.tiktok.com/@jeannestjames

facebook.com/JeanneStJamesAuthor
amazon.com/author/jeannestjames
instagram.com/JeanneStJames
bookbub.com/authors/jeanne-st-james
goodreads.com/JeanneStJames
pinterest.com/JeanneStJames

Get a FREE Sampler Book

This book contains the first chapter of a variety of my books. This will give you a taste of the type of books I write and if you enjoy the first chapter, I hope you'll be interested in reading the rest of the book.

Each book I list in the sampler will include the description of the book, the genre, and the first chapter, along with links to find out more. I hope you find a book you will enjoy curling up with!

Get it here: BookHip.com/MTQQKK